The Road to LaGrange

A Sanctuary Story

Kerry L. Malone

The Road to LaGrange

Published by Sanctuary Books, Houston, TX
Printed in the United States of America
First edition, 2023

ISBN: 979-8-9886428-3-1
eBook ISBN: 979-8-9886428-6-2
Library of Congress Control Number: 2023922597

Cover design by Suzie Blackwell Design

This novel is dedicated to the memory of John Lee Wallace. He was the best friend a man could have and has always been the inspiration for the character of Fat Sally Lombardo in this story and in my other books.

Prologue

I provide this bit of text by way of explanation or, possibly, as an apology to the one of my favorite places in my favorite state. LaGrange, Texas has been special to me since the first time I crossed the Colorado and rode up the hill with my parents in our 1949 Dodge. That was probably sometime in 1954, but I couldn't be sure. We took lots of Sunday drives and Monument Hill was on our route more than once.

Most of this story is set in and around LaGrange and in other parts of Fayette County. I hope that any reader who is familiar with the area will find that I have tried to capture the essence of the place but understand that I have taken some liberties with geography and typography. This was done to satisfy the needs of the story and I hope it doesn't take away from anyone's enjoyment. If you have never been there, it's a worthwhile side trip. Nothing dramatic—just a slice of Texas that I find special.

None of the characters in the story have any connection to anyone, living or dead. They are entirely from my own imagination and should not reflect on any of the fine public servants or citizens of the communities in the story. The same is true for any incidents described. Some actual locations—buildings, businesses and the like—were used but most were fictional.

The other location with a role in the story is the River Walk, in San Antonio. Some places described there are fictional and others are real or based on real locations. None of the events described are from reality.

Disclaimers out of the way, I hope you enjoy taking

Highway 71 to LaGrange with Doc and Fat Sally.

KLM

The Road to LaGrange

1.

As a man gets older, he needs to face the fact that things change. Some change faster than others. Aging is a continuing process of loss. The man doesn't even notice he has lost some things until long after they are gone. Time's theft of bits and pieces from one's physical body is sinister. Other changes come with impact that stuns the man, immediately and forever.

Everyone called him Doc—his name was Connor Quinn—and he knew loss. When he was a boy, his state trooper father died in his cruiser at a railroad crossing on a foggy morning. He lost his school teacher mother to cancer while he was in college—a horrid, lengthy, painful way to leave the world—and misery for loved ones to witness.

His only passion as a young man had been football, and he lost that. The loss came more slowly, the result of injuries and, if he were to be honest with himself, from his own lack of skill. He didn't fully accept this loss until years after his playing days were over, and then it came almost as a surprise. He never got past scanning the horizon for the stadium lights when he drove into a new town.

He made the conscious decision to leave his studies for a doctorate in physics because he had just lost interest—in both the subject and his fellow scholars. He didn't regard this as a loss but an act of self-determination. Around the same time, his first marriage died, he fell in love and got involved in the motorcycle culture. He was a founding member of a new motorcycle club—Thursday's Children. He lost that, as well. It ended dramatically in a campground on Petit Jean Mountain in the Ozarks. The fact that he made the decision for it to end didn't erase the loss or his biker attitude—or, at least, part of it. The scar left by certain things is as indelible as a tattoo—Marine, Aggie, Eagle Scout, musician, biker . . .

The greatest loss Doc suffered was the death of his second wife, Kay. It was immediate and final. On a beautiful Sunday ride on his Harley, they were struck by a lady driving to her grandson's birthday party. Kay died at the scene, looking into Doc's eyes. This loss would be with him for the rest of his life. He was only twenty-eight at the time. He loved Kay without limit and would never know that love again, in his long but mostly solitary life.

One thing that Doc never lost was his best friend. Through whatever life dealt, Fat Sally was Doc's friend. His name was Salvatore Lombardo, and his personality was as expansive as his bulk. In spite of his name, he was half Scott and half Italian. They met in 1972, when both dipped their toes into the biker life, and they remained brothers even though they only wore club colors for two years. They always stood back-to-back to take on all challenges. And side by side, devouring what pleasures the world offered.

***

"You ready for another cold one?" Fat Sally wanted to know. The Texas sun was lifting waves of heat from the hills as he drove his Ford van along the way to Marble Falls. No air conditioning—it died a year before and Sally could afford the heat better than he could the price of repairs.

Doc tossed his cigarette butt out the van's window and then thought better of it. He hoped he hadn't just caused the dry weeds along the road to explode. "Damn! I shouldn't have done that," he said, looking back. "Yeah, I'll have another one and I guess you will too." He reached between the captain's chairs and pulled two Shiners from the Coleman. Not Shiner Bock—but honest-to-God beer, in clear bottles, famous for each one in a six-pack having a little different hue. Strong, lots of hops, like the old men in the domino parlors drank. The church key was tied to the cooler with a string. He used it to pop the tops and watched some of the foam spill on the dirty blue plush carpet of the old hippie van. He handed one bottle to his friend and took a long pull from his own. Sweating like they were, the beer would go through them without causing much of a buzz even though they had been going into the cooler every few minutes.

"You know, the rumor is that the fucking state is about to pass an open container law. I always thought Texas would never have income tax or open container laws. They pass either one of them and there will be a turnover in the damn capital. Bunch of fuckin' politicians gonna have to go to work for a living." said Sal as he chugged his Shiner. "Hell of a thing when a man can't have a beer driving home from work after a hard day." He need not have worried. This was 1996 and it would still be several years before open containers would be banned. State income tax would never plague residents of the Lone Star State.

Doc and Fat Sally were making their annual 'runaway'—this time it was to try to get a bottle of wine from every vineyard within driving distance. Wineries were still in their infancy in most of the state and Doc wanted to see if they might give him a place to invest. Investment or not, it would be fun driving around and tasting some free wine.

This year, their choices for their runaway theme were wine, barbeque, tacos, border town whorehouses, or offshore fishing—several of these would have been replays of previous get-aways. The Texas Wine Tour won out. They didn't make the decision until after they left Sal's house in Deer Park. The big man was leaning toward a revised Texas Taco Tour—"Where everything we eat is either in a tortilla or, at least looks like a taco," was how he described the rules. Good Mexican food was easy to find where both of them lived—Doc in San Antonio and Sal in the Houston suburb. And finding something that resembled a taco wasn't an issue for either of them. Sal was married but his wife, Lois, gave him a lot of room where other women were concerned, and he did the same for her with men. Doc's wife had been killed twenty years earlier and he would never remarry. He had no issues with seeking pleasures of the flesh and, in general, women responded to him.

Passing through Houston, after leaving Sally's house, they stopped at Spec's and surveyed bottles for Texas wineries. Sally even made notes in his draftsman's precise script. They took the Rand McNally out of the glove box and charted their route.

It was mid-afternoon, so they only drove as far as LaGrange, where they spent the night at a cheap motel near the banks of the Colorado. Doc had loved the little town since his first visit there many years earlier. It was an interesting place with an interesting history. Located at the southeast edge of the Texas Hill Country, it had been founded in the 1820s as a fort on the Colorado River of Texas. It had been populated by German and Czech settlers later in that century and took on many of their traditions. On a bluff overlooking the town, historically minded Texans had established the Monument Hill site, adjacent to an old brewery. The state erected a tall, handsome monument, and a crypt honoring heroes of Texas' post-revolution period.

The town had also been the home of the infamous Chicken Ranch, a brothel that had operated, mostly out in the open, for around seventy years. The uproar created by a Houston sensationalist newscaster, in the 1970s, had brought on its demise. The events surrounding this period were the basis for the play and movie called "The Best Little

Whorehouse in Texas."

The town was pretty and serene and off the beaten path. A visit there always brought Doc peace.

They rose before daylight the next morning and drove to the Courthouse Square where they bought fresh kolaches—two each, poppy seed and prune—at the little bakery operated by two old Czech ladies. They crossed the US 77 bridge, and the van climbed the curving highway and turned right at the road leading to Monument Hill. It wasn't yet daylight, and the park wasn't open yet. They stepped across a low barrier and walked to the edge of the cliff, carrying bottles of Shiner and the bag of kolaches. They sat on a concrete bench, had their breakfast, and washed the Czech pastries down with beer in the morning mist.

"You know, when I die, I think I want to have my ashes sprinkled off the cliff here. This is one of my favorite places in Texas," said Doc, as he surveyed the bend in the river and town far below.

Sal thought about it for only a beat before saying, "Well, I hope you leave them instructions to wait for a good south breeze before tossing you out. Anything else and you'd wind up back in their faces." They both laughed.

They finished their breakfast and Sal rolled a thin joint and fired it up, took a deep toke and handed it to Doc, who followed suit. Just then, they heard a car slide to a stop in the parking lot. Doc saw it from the corner of his eye. They heard the door slam a man's voice scream in Spanish. They watched as a young woman in a loose-fitting blue dress ran past the monument to the Dawson Massacre and Black Bean Detail. She clambered over the retaining wall and ran to the edge of the cliff and disappeared. The car sped out of the lot, its tires blasting gravel, the man still yelling, "*Puta*!"

"What the fuck!?" said Doc as the two men stood and rushed to the edge of the abyss. They looked over, the best they could without crossing the low rock wall. Then Doc climbed over and peered down.

"I can't see her. Can you?" asked Sal.

"I think I see something down in the trees. Shit, I think she's caught in the branches of one of the trees down there. What the hell should we do?"

They turned to see a Park Ranger pulling into the lot by the park's office. He headed down the path as fast as he could, without running. As he got closer to Doc and Sal, it was evident that he was not pleased. Still thirty feet away, he spoke loudly, "What are you old boys doing out here this early. You know, we ain't opened up the park yet."

Sal said, "Hey man, you need to take a look at this. Some chick jumped over the cliff. I think she's hung up in the trees down below."

"What the hell?" said the ranger and followed them to the edge of the drop off. He carefully climbed over the low wall, kept one hand on it and leaned over as far as he dared. He took off his hat so he could see better—or so he wouldn't drop it over the edge—and handed it back to Doc. He stood there for a minute, gazing down. "Shit! I think you're right. There's something down there. What did y'all have to do with this?"

"Nothing, man! We were just having our breakfast and enjoying the morning when this chick comes running from a car and just goes over," replied Sal.

"I don't see no car. Just some damn hippie-looking van."

"Van's mine, dammit! Some guy was hollering and drove away fast when the girl jumped," said Sal.

"Well, y'all can just cool your wheels for a while. I have to call the Sheriff. You two don't go no place."

"Yeah, OK," said Sal.

He and Doc exchanged looks and walked to cliff's edge and looked down again. Doc lit a Marlboro, shaking his head. In a low voice, he said, "What did you do with that doobie? Cops are coming and you don't want them seeing that. Rural Texas is still not a place where they take smoking dope lightly."

"No, man! I flipped that over the edge—it was almost gone, anyway—but I ain't tossing my baggie. Tucked it in my boot after I rolled the joint. Unless they strip search us, we are gonna be OK." As they walked back to their bench, Sal looked at Doc the way he always did and said, "How do you smoke them nasty bastards?"

"I always like to have me a smoke after I have a smoke. And after breakfast most days and always after I watch somebody commit sideways."

It took the Sheriff twenty minutes to get to the park. A deputy, actually wearing a fine straw cowboy hat, gold-colored badge, and a Model 1911 on his hip. The deputy and the park ranger spoke for a few minutes by the entrance, the ranger pointing at Doc and Sal and toward the jumping off point. Then they walked to the wall and the deputy climbed over and carefully looked down and shook his head. Then they walked to the bench where the Doc and Sal waited.

"What can you two tell me about what's going on here? Tell me what happened, in your own words," said the deputy.

Doc, wondering who else's words he would use, said, "We were just having breakfast here before hitting the road and this car pulled into the lot and a young woman jumped out and ran to the edge and disappeared. The guy in the car hauled ass. He was hollering at the girl, calling her a '*puta*' but we didn't really get a look at him. I didn't understand the other stuff he was yelling but Sal may have. He has better Spanish than me."

The deputy looked over at the empty beer bottles and the crumpled kolache bag. "What in the hell were you doing here, in the first place. You know, it ain't legal for y'all to be in here before the place opens to the public. And it damn sure ain't legal to be consuming alcohol in the park—open or closed, the park, that is." Doc and Sal just looked at each other, Sal smiling and holding his laughter in respect for the law.

"You two show me some ID. Who the hell are you?"

"My name is Salvatore Lombardo and I live in Deer Park. We're just off on a run-away. Wanted to visit some wineries and shit. We sort of do this a couple of times a year. Not always looking for wine. Sometimes we are looking for other stuff." He handed his driver's license to the officer. Doc did the same.

"How about you?" said the deputy, looking at Doc.

"I'm Connor Quinn but most folks call me Doc. I work for an oilfield supply outfit. I live in San Antonio." What he didn't say was that he was his company's Vice President, in charge of four states.

"OK. Big guy, what do you do for a living? When you ain't hunting for 'wineries' I mean? You look like some kind of biker of something."

Sal was about to develop an attitude, but he just kept smiling. He could see how the deputy might get that impression since he was wearing overalls, a black T-shirt, a WFO Choppers gimmie cap, and heavy boots. "I'm a piping design draftsman. I freelance. And it ain't against no laws to be a biker, is it? I used to be one, but not anymore, I guess."

"Y'all don't get no ideas about going nowhere. I need to get the Sheriff out here and we need to figure out what to do about the woman. She may be just injured or something."

Doc and Sal looked at each other, shaking their heads. They saw no movement from the figure that appeared to be lodged in the branches of the water oaks at the bottom of the two-hundred-foot drop.

While they were waiting, the deputy draped yellow and black crime scene tape across the entry to the park and between the tall monument and the rock wall at the cliff's edge. The ranger put up a sign at the entrance to the parking lot, announcing that Monument Hill was closed today. Then he got on the phone and made some official calls, alerting the other park workers of the incident and notifying Parks and Wildlife in Austin.

When Sheriff Hillman arrived, the introductions were again exchanged, and he led Doc and Sal into the park office building. They took seats in a small meeting room and the Sheriff said, "OK now boys, tell me what you told Deputy Schaer. And don't skip nothing."

They told the same story as they told earlier, almost word for word. When they finished, Hillman asked, "You say a guy in a car dropped the girl off. And you didn't see him but you saw the car. What kind was it?"

Doc and Sal hadn't discussed it before, and both looked a little confused. Then Doc said, "If I had to guess, I'd say it was maybe a late 70s Chevy Monte Carlo or, maybe, an Impala 2-door? It was still kind of dark out. What do you think, Sal?"

"Could be—I didn't really see it."

Doc said, "All the damn GM cars looked about the same back then. Caddies look about the same as a Monte Carlo. Could have been something later, maybe? It was dark colored. Black maybe, or dark blue? It wasn't anything new, anyway."

"Y'all are a hell of a lot of help! Big man, can you even see anything with them thick specs? Anything else you can remember?"

"Don't worry about what Sal can see. He sees just fine. The guy was talking Spanish. Kept hollering '*puta*' at the girl. He just jumped out of the car and right back in before he drove away." said Doc.

"That's how I heard it. I think he was telling her to come back. Something like 'get your ass back in the car' best I could understand. He was cussing a lot—*chinga* this and *chinga* that. And calling her a whore—*puta*."

Just as Sal finished talking, there was a knock on the room's door and a trooper in full State Police regalia walked in without being invited. His insignia indicated he was no normal highway patrolman. Doc often worked with the state guys for company vehicle wrecks and robberies of company equipment. He recognized the officer to be a Major by the gold leaves on his shoulders. The Major removed his cowboy hat and placed it crown-down on the conference table. The Sheriff introduced him as John Naiser. Once again, Sal and Doc had to relate their story for the Major's benefit.

After the third telling of the events, Naiser said, "You boys sit tight while the grownups have a little talk." Doc and Sal both chuckled at the reference and the three law enforcement guys walked out and closed the door.

"What the fuck you suppose that's all about?" asked Sal.

"Man, you got me. They can't possibly think we have anything to do with this. Do you think? Hell, any self-respecting guilty man would have run like hell—just like the guy in the car did."

When the lawmen came back into the room, Sheriff Hillman was the first to speak. "Look. We don't have nothing we can charge you boys with right now, but you need to stick around LaGrange until we say you can go. You got that. We need you just to sit tight in here for a while longer, but you need to plan to stay in the area. No goin' back to San Antone or Houston or no place. We could charge you with trespass on state property but, since you are the only witnesses, we don't want to be assholes on that one."

"Shit! We had plans for a little holiday. This is bullshit! We told you everything we know. Why don't you just let us go on our way?" Sally was getting agitated and his face was turning red as he laid his best 'go to hell' scowl on the cops—and he had that look mastered.

Doc knew Sal's moods and he held up his hand and said, "Settle down Sal. Hey guys, my old man was a state trooper. He got killed in the line of duty when I was just a little kid. I respect y'all and I respect the law. Thanks for not giving us a ticket for being in the park."

The park ranger piped up, "And for not charging you for bringing beer in this sacred place!"

Doc nodded. "We can probably stay in the same dump as last night. It didn't look like a place that fills up very often."

Naiser spoke up, "We are going to need to check out your vehicle. That van in the lot is yours. Right? Anyway, do you give us permission to take a look inside? If not, we can get a warrant pretty quick."

Their minds worked quickly. *What did we leave in the van that we don't want the law to see?* Sally took off his thick glasses and wiped the lenses as they looked into one another's eyes, communicating in the unspoken language they had developed over the past twenty-plus years. The only real contraband they had was on Sal's person—a little bag of pot and papers in his boot and two hits of ecstasy—what Sally called 'St. Joseph baby acid'—in one of the little pockets on his overalls. He answered for the two of them, "I guess that will be OK. We ain't got nothing to hide. I'm telling you now, there is a .45, almost like the one the deputy carries, in the glove box and there is a cooler full of Shiner and Lone Star, and a fifth of tequila in the cooler. Ain't none of that against the law, far as I know." He tossed the Sheriff his keys.

Hillman nodded at Naiser who said, "I have a couple of officers who will look through the van while y'all cool it in here. We have some troopers and a couple of local boys down in the woods now trying to retrieve the woman. You boys can amuse yourselves here for a couple of hours."

Sal crossed his huge arms across his chest, breathing heavily through his nose—obviously not happy but resigned to his fate. He slid the bill of his cap down over his eyes and sagged down in his chair. Doc just leaned back and said, "Y'all got any of them parks magazines or maybe a Texas Highways or Texas Monthly for us to read while we are waiting. Boring as hell, just sitting and waiting."

The ranger said, "I'll find y'all some reading material. Just sit tight. Would you like some coffee or something while you wait?"

Sal brightened, looking up just enough for his tormenters to see his glaring eyes, "Can you bring our cooler in so we can at least have a beer?"

The ranger just smiled and said, "Now, you know we can't have that in here. This is a historical site so have some respect." Sal lowered his chin to his chest again and all the constabulary made their exit.

When they were out of earshot, Doc said, "You sure there's nothing in the van to get us busted? I'm too damn old to go to jail for a seed or something."

"No, man! I even vacuumed the old bus out so you wouldn't get your fucking jeans dirty riding around backwoods of Texas. Even took it to the car wash for its annual bath! You can almost see the paint job now." He thought for a few seconds and continued, "We should have raised more of a stink. This shit ain't right. If we had just hauled ass after the bitch jumped, we'd be drinking free wine samples by now."

"Did you check the ashtray for roaches? I think we

put a little one in there yesterday on the drive."

"Shit, man! I ate that this morning in the middle of a prune kolache."

"OK, I forgot you'd eat any goddamn thing. I thought eating a roach went out in about 1975."

"Well, maybe for everybody else."

A few minutes later, a lady they didn't recognize delivered a stack of magazines—National Geographics, Texas Monthly, and Texas Highways. "Mr. Stamper—Ranger Stamper—asked me to let you fellows have these. Now, y'all bring them back to the reception area when y'all are done, will you please. Bless your hearts! I heard what happened. That must have been just awful." She closed the door and was gone. Sal was napping in his chair before she got back to her desk. Doc found a Texas Highways he hadn't read and was learning about the Luling Watermelon Thump celebration.

***

2.

It was almost noon before anyone came back into the room. Deputy Schaer walked in and tossed Sal his keys and said, "State boys said your damn vehicle smelled like a opium den but they couldn't find nothin' to put you in jail."

Sal gave him a hard look and said, "Yeah, when I bought the van, it smelled that way. Can't seem to get the stink out. It was cheap and maybe that's why. Always wondered what they had been doing in there."

"Yeah, right. Anyway, I need to know where you are staying until we let you go. If we let you go, I mean," said Schaer.

Sal looked at Doc and asked, "Do you remember the name of the place?" Then, looking at the deputy, "It's run by a family of Indians or something—dot, not feather. Hell, I never paid no attention to the sign."

Doc spoke, "I think it's called Riverside or something like that."

"Yeah, I know the place. It's called Riverview Motel. What a fucking dump!" the Deputy told them. "We got the description of your van, and our boys will be watching for y'all to try to leave town. That old thing sticks out like a sore thumb. We ought to arrest you just for driving somethin like that," and he laughed, turned, and walked out.

As he was going, Sal hollered, "Hey! Is there any place worth a shit to eat around here?"

The deputy stuck his head back in the door and said, "This is Friday and there's an old man who sells some seriously good barbeque on Fridays and Saturdays, out of a trailer pit he parks just across the river—north bridge. The Mexican joint on that same road ain't bad and there is a great truck stop kind of place close by the high school on the main drag. Great kolaches but not as good as the Kopecky sisters sell on the square."

"Yep, them old ladies make some fine kolaches. We got some there this morning before daylight. That's been a while and I could eat the ass end of mule about now. Doc, let's find some groceries," said Sal.

Doc dropped the magazines back on the lady's desk as they walked past, and she smiled. They followed the deputy out of the building and walked over to Sal's van. When they got in, the first thing Sal did was turn around and take a look inside the cooler. "Goddamnit! I think them state cops pilfered some of our damn beer."

"Come on, man. They wouldn't do nothing like that." Doc turned to look into the cooler and said, "Sally, you just forgot how much beer we drank on the drive up here. They didn't steal any."

"Well, I'm not so sure. You gotta watch those bastards every minute."

He started the van and they drove back out of the lot and down the hill toward the Colorado River bridge. They looked to the left along the river bank and saw several squad cars, a couple of trucks and an ambulance, all there to retrieve the young woman's body from the trees. They could hear what sounded like chain saws buzzing in the distance. Sal said, "Wonder what they are going to find when they get the girl to the coroner." Doc just shrugged his shoulders and kept watching until they were out of sight.

They turned left at the light at the end of the bridge and Sal pointed at the café that the deputy said was a truck stop. Just a couple of hundred yards away was the Riverview, where they pulled into the lot and parked by the office. When they walked in, the overwhelming aroma of curry hit them in the face like a heavy pillow—not a bad smell, but powerful. From their stay the previous night, they knew curry went no further than the office and proprietor's living quarters adjacent to the office.

"Oh, you back again! Good. Or did you leave something here?"

"No, we need to stay a while longer. We could use the same room as last night or another one with two beds," Doc said and pushed his American Express card across the desk.

"That room was cleaned so you can have it again if it was suitable to you. How many nights do you need the room?"

"That room's fine. Right now, we don't know how long we will need to stay, so just keep the ticket open, will you."

As the proprietor was taking care of the business end of his business, he wanted to make small talk. "Did you hear? A girl jumped off the cliff across the river. It is the talk of the town. Nothing like that ever happens in LaGrange. This is a very quiet town."

"Seems we might have heard something about that," said Sal as he and Doc exchanged glances.

They took the room keys and pulled the van to the spot in front of Room 29. Walking in, Sal said, "I'm damn glad the rooms don't smell like the office. About fifteen minutes of that and I'd puke. And I like Indian food."

"This place isn't too bad. We have definitely stayed in worse. What is the worst place you figure you ever spent the night?" Doc wanted to know.

Sally thought for a moment and said, "You mean, besides in the Nam? I was in some pretty rank places there. Some were paid for by our Uncle and some not."

"No man, you can't count that shit. I mean in the world—outside of your unfortunate southeast Asia vacation."

"Well, we spent the night in that whorehouse in Villa Acuna. The sheets were pretty clean—didn't look like they'd been used but a time or two—and it was comfortable with the windows open. Circulation of the air is important in a place like that. I don't know that we slept much that night so maybe it don't count."

"You are forgetting one. How about Albino Bob's 'guest room'? Hey, at least we didn't have to collect the dead rats and dried up condoms in these fleabag motels."

"Well, I'm not gonna look under the bed. Man, I'm starving to death. Let's go get something to eat," said Sal and they walked back out to the van. "Let's see if we can find that man with the barbeque trailer. They said it was just across the north bridge."

The drive took them past the county courthouse and town square where things were very quiet on a Friday afternoon in the summer. Through the domino parlor windows, they could see the old men with their beer and games of Moon and 42. Those places were air conditioned. If they had stopped and gone inside, they would have still heard Czech and German being spoken. Even in 1996, the traditions of the old countries had not totally disappeared, but they were fading fast. When these old men were kids, they had lived in homes where English wasn't spoken and many never learned until it was forced on them by the schools. Even people the same age as Sally and Doc had to learn the new language when they arrived, ill-prepared, for the first grade. It was that way in large sections of Central Texas.

As they drove across the north bridge, they saw a big pull-behind pit and a folding table laid out on a patch of bare ground. There were two cars parked by the table and the pitmaster was slicing from a huge chunk of meat the color of dark chocolate. They knew that was what they were looking for. Just as they exited the bridge, an old rusty red Ford 150 passed them, heading toward town. They both noticed when the truck swerved and its two right wheels hit the dirt and gravel on the roadside before it righted and continued on its way but moving very slowly. Sal thought he saw the man on the passenger side craning his head out of his window, looking at the van.

"What the fuck you suppose that was about?" Doc wanted to know.

"Looked like a couple of mojados to me, brother. Probably got off early on a Friday and were already into the cerveza. I'm just glad they didn't run into us. That would have fucked up an already fucked up day."

They pulled up behind the two cars already stopped at the rolling smoker and waited until two ladies, who obviously knew the proprietor, got their orders rolled in brick red butcher paper. "What can I do for you fellers?" the pitmaster asked.

"Whatcha got?" Fat Sally wanted to know.

"Still got some brisket but it's going fast. Got a shoulder clod I haven't sliced yet. Smoked all night and up to now, today. I like it better than brisket anyway. Got some good sausage, made in Lockhart. Same folks that make the rings for Kreuz Market. Can't beat that. So, what will you boys have?"

They mulled the selections and asked him to slice them a pound and a half of shoulder clod and two of the little sausage rings. The old man was proud of his barbeque and the order cost almost $20 but he threw in four slices of white bread and some crinkle-cut pickles and a handful of jalapenos. He wrapped it all in the same butcher paper as he had used for the ladies and the grease was showing on the outside before they got the package back into the van. Doc put it on top of the Coleman cooler so as not to soil the already disgusting blue shag on the floor.

Sal wheeled the van around and drove back across the bridge. When they passed the 7-Eleven store just over the bridge, they noticed the rusty Ford truck parked beside the phone booth. Both of the truck's passengers were standing by the phone. One was on the phone with his hands gesturing like he thought the party on the other end of the line could see him. Both men stared at the van as it rolled past and that wasn't lost on Doc and Sal.

"What the fuck is up with them boys? They seem mighty interested in us," Doc wondered.

"Fuck um! Let's find a place to eat. We got any beer left?"

They saw a sign for the city park and drove by. There was a swimming pool and two ballparks but no tables or benches. "Hell, let's just find a place in the shade in that baseball park," Sal suggested and that's what they did. The sun was sinking low by then and both men were famished, having eaten nothing since their kolaches and beer breakfast.

They sat under the tin roof that covered the bleachers. Summer sounds echoed from happy kids at the swimming pool. They unfolded the meat and found the bread slices already soaked in grease, but they didn't care. Both pulled their knives from their pockets and made quick work of the beef and sausage. The little sausages rings were so well done that the casing was crisp and squirted grease when poked and the taste was redolent with garlic and black pepper. Sally bit a hunk of jalapeno between each bite of meat and squinched his face as it turned red. "These some damn spicy peppers! You need to have some before I eat um all."

"Thanks but no-thanks. I'll stick to pickles. You go ahead and burn yourself down with them damn jalapenos. They will pay you a visit again in the morning. I ain't as tough as you."

They finished eating and washed off at the hydrant beside one of the dugouts and shook their hands dry as best they could, finally giving up and wiping water off on their pants. Sal wasn't concerned with the way his overalls looked but Doc grimaced as he finished the job on his razor-creased Wranglers.

"What should we do now. Sure as hell ain't ready to call it a night. Hell, it's not even night yet anyway," said Doc.

"Let's find us a honkytonk with a good air conditioner and just kick back for a while. Drink some beer. Maybe run into a graduate of the Chicken Ranch. Can't never tell."

"OK, let's see what LaGrange has to offer. But, hey! Anything left over from the Chicken Ranch is older and probably uglier than we are. That place was shut down over twenty years ago."

"Doc, you know, my standards ain't the same as yours. Long as it's still breathin', it's fair game."

They drove back to the courthouse square and decided to stop at the Riverview and freshen up a bit, in case any Chicken Ranch wannabes were on the menu for the evening. Sal even put on a clean T-shirt. By the time they were back in the van, it was almost full dark outside. They pulled out of the lot and Doc noticed the red pickup parked at the truck stop cafe. Only one man was in it but he was looking at them as they drove by. Doc didn't want to mention it to Sal because he knew that might lead to a confrontation. Probably just a coincidence, Doc thought.

On the east edge of town, they found a likely looking beer joint with a sign that said 'Starters' in faded neon. It was nestled back in a grove of oaks with a dozen or so vehicles in the gravel lot—mostly pickups but one Corvette. When they walked in the place, it was dark and private with a jukebox for entertainment. They ordered Lone Stars and found an empty table. Most of the crowd looked to be farmers or construction workers. There were four women, but they were with men and three would have held no interest for Doc, anyway. Sal, well maybe. One of the men was dressed in a sport coat and open collar shirt and he was sitting with a strikingly beautiful woman. They took for granted that he was the Corvette. The music coming from the speakers wasn't bad—mostly current country and old rock. Doc lit a Marlboro and, for the first time since the girl jumped, he felt completely relaxed.

When they were on their second beer, the barroom door opened and Deputy Schaer and another officer, who they hadn't seen before, walked in. Schaer scanned the room and nodded at Mr. Corvette. Then he walked directly to Doc and Sal's table. He was slightly built, with tight eyes, thinning hair, and a pasty face. Doc thought he always looked like he had smelled something offensive. Probably got beat up a lot as a kid. A few people in the beer joint looked at the officers when they walked toward the two big strangers but lost interest quickly and went back to their beer and conversation. Schaer said, "I've been looking all over for y'all. Thought you left town and I might need to put out an APB on you."

Sal looked up from his beer and said, "Been right here, just like you said. Got a room at the Shitterview and ate barbeque over at the little league park. Why you lookin' for us?"

Schaer pulled up a chair, turned it around, and straddled it leaning his elbows on the chair back. He thought he was looking all macho. "We got some information about the girl and thought you deserved to know, seeing how y'all saw her go over."

Both men muttered an unenthusiastic "OK" and the

Deputy continued, speaking low.

"Yeah, it ain't pretty and y'all ain't out of the woods yet. She was dead when they cut her out of the branches of a tree. Her neck was broke. But the interesting part is that she had been tied up or something. What they call ligature marks around her wrists and ankles. Also had cigarette burns on her back but they were old scars. Don't know for sure yet but they are testing her for sexual mistreatment but had to send her body to Austin for that. She's headed that direction right now." Then he looked around to make sure nobody else could hear and continued, "I ain't supposed to mention this but she had needle tracks on her arms and, maybe, between her toes. They will do some kind of investigation to check on that."

Doc said, "Damn! That sounds grim. Did she have any ID on her?"

"Barely had any clothes on. Just that little dress thing y'all saw her in and a pair of huaraches. No underwear or nothin'."

Sal asked, "Y'all find anything about the car?"

Schaer cocked his head to the side and said, "What? With that great description y'all gave us. Maybe a Chevy, maybe a Caddy, maybe any goddamn thing. No, we ain't even tried to follow up on the car. Maybe if y'all was a little more observant."

"Anything we can do to help?" asked Doc.

"Just don't go no place until we tell you that you can. And try not to get into trouble. Don't get in no fights or nothin'. Y'all are big ol' boys but these Bohunks will kick your ass."

"Yeah, well I guess we are just too old for that kind of shit. We ain't bothering nobody and if y'all hadn't got in our way we'd be someplace else not bothering somebody else," Sal replied as the officers walked toward the door,

Schaer waving as he left.

When they were gone, Doc asked, "What do you make of that? Sounds like the girl was being held hostage or something. People that do something like that need a good killin'."

"I hear you, brother. There's lots of pieces of shit breathing up good air in this world." Sal replied and shook his head. "Let's go riding and I'll roll us one for the road. We can kinda drive around in the country and smoke it. Don't want to do that in town. Shit! They're already looking for a reason to fuck with us."

***

3.

"You drive while I roll," said Sal as they walked toward the van and Doc got in the driver side with Sal in the passenger seat. He strained to reach his boot, cussing, "Shit! I shoulda got the baggie before I sat down. Can't reach my foot 'cause my belly's too big." Doc laughed and Sally said, "Fuck you!" and, after a lot of grunting, extracted the baggie. Doc drove northeast along the state highway toward Giddings while Sal rolled up his window so as not to lose any of the precious shake to the elements. When he was done, he smiled and proudly held up a perfect, fat joint for Doc to appreciate.

"Nice! Now fire that mutha up," said Doc. "I do appreciate your rolling skills since I can't roll worth a shit. Never have."

They drove along and smoked their doobie and life was good. They stopped at a tumble-down little beer joint at a wide spot in the road called Warda. There were only two old trucks parked by the building. When they walked in, all eyes in the place—or what eyes there were—turned to them but nobody looked hostile. In fact, they looked friendly. There was a septuagenarian lady with a bun and a pair of pink capri pants behind the slab of a bar.

"How you boys doin'? What can I get you?" she asked.

"We fine. Be finer with a couple of Lone Stars," said Sally. He listed just a bit, trying to get his balance because the floor was tilted considerably toward the back wall of the building. He knew the pot wasn't that good.

"Well now, I can't serve no Lone Star because we are

fresh out. How 'bout a Shiner or Bud?"

"Give us one of each," said Doc and they stood by the bar while Doc chose the Shiner and Sal took the Bud. The reason they stood by the bar was because both of the tables in the place were occupied. One of the men seated at a table with an elderly woman and a younger man got up and walked over to them.

"You old boys ain't from around here, are you? Welcome to the Warda bar," he said, putting out his weathered hand to shake. Both did. "Where y'all from and what are you doin' in this neck of the woods?"

Sally immediately began to develop an attitude and Doc recognized the signs. He stepped forward and said, "Yes sir! My name is Quinn and this here is Lombardo. We are just passing through. Doin' some business in LaGrange and just went for a drive to check out the sights."

"Well, y'all enjoy yourselves. Hey, when you get done with your beer you can just drop the bottle on the floor and it will roll back to the wall. Florence don't mind picking um up," he said and cackled as he walked back to his table.

Florence just smiled and said, "Now Curtis, don't you be like that! I'll bar you from the place again." All the locals laughed until they cried, and Doc and Sal saw the humor but guessed you had be from there to get the full impact of the joke. When they finished their beer, Doc sat his empty on the bar, but Sally gently dropped his on the floor and watched as it meandered its way to the back wall and settled with a light clink.

Back in the van with Doc again behind the wheel, Sal said, "You know, lots of folks are living just like them. Don't go no place except the little honkytonk and don't know nobody except the locals. You think you could live that kind of life?"

"I don't think so. Seems like I've been in perpetual motion since I left Sanctuary. Hell, even before that. I think all the quiet would drive me fucking nuts."

"I don't know, brother. Maybe I could enjoy a little quiet. There ain't none of that at my house or where I'm living. Might be just the change I need."

Doc drove out of the little lot and turned back toward LaGrange. They didn't talk much but they really didn't need to.

***

When they turned onto the main drag and drove past the courthouse square, there was a bit of Friday night traffic. Normal, with local kids out for fun and adults finishing a long day and going home. A block past the courthouse, a Chevrolet sedan pulled in behind them. As he was about to turn into Riverview Motel, Doc thought he saw the old red pickup across the street and just around the corner, facing the motel.

"Sally, wake up! We're almost home."

"I ain't sleeping. Just resting my eyes. You wanna do that 'X' tonight or save in case we ever get the fuck out of LaGrange."

"No, man! I ain't wanting to stay up half the night all fucked up. Let's do it while we are riding in the hill country—like you say, if we ever get the fuck out of LaGrange."

As Doc stopped in front of room 29 and shifted into park, the first of nine shots split the quiet LaGrange night. Sal moved faster than a man his size should. He opened the glove box and pulled out his .45 as he rolled out and onto the ground.

Doc ducked low behind his drive-side door and heard bullets slamming into the metal. There was no place for him to go. Then he heard seven loud explosions from right below where he crouched. It was Fat Sally emptying the clip of his Model 1911. He couldn't see the shooters and was just firing in their general direction, but it was enough. They heard tires screaming and all went silent again.

"You OK Doc?" Sally wanted to know.

"Holy shit! I think so. How are you?"

"No harm. Busted my ass falling on the fucking gravel and knocked the shit out of my head trying to get under the fucking van. That didn't work."

The sirens of two town cops and one deputy sheriff descended on the motel as some of the guests peered out to see what all the excitement was about. Others hid. The proprietor, wearing some kind of sleeping garment, was wringing his hands and standing in the office doorway.

After some difficulty, Doc was able to get the door open and he climbed carefully out of the van. He looked himself up and down and saw no blood. He looked in the side-view mirror and brushed his hair back. Sal limped around the front of the van, his pistol still in his hand, slide back on the empty clip. Sal's right side overall strap had pulled its button off and was hanging, and his knees were scuffed. They just looked at each other.

"Drop the gun or I'll shoot!" It was a pot-bellied, older city cop, holding an ancient Smith and Wesson with both hands. Sal dropped his gun and they both held their hands up. "Down on your knees!"

Sally shook his head and glared at the cop. "I ain't getting on my knees for nobody, so you can just settle down. Somebody was shooting at us so just fuck off."

Sheriff Hillman, himself, was walking from the street, toward the van, with a shotgun in his hand. "Allen, it's OK. These guys look like the victims here. Let me take it from here. I know these guys."

The cop, Allen, looked over his shoulder, still holding his gun on Doc and Sal. "Sheriff, this is a city matter."

"It's OK. Come over here for a minute and I'll let you know about these guys." The cop lowered his gun but didn't holster it. He backed up and Hillman put an arm around the cop's shoulder.

"Look Sheriff, my Chief ain't gonna be too happy about you taking jurisdiction on this," said Officer Allen.

"I appreciate you getting here so fast. That was good and probably kept things from escalating. Let me talk to the Chief. This started outside the city limits, with the Monument Hill mess this morning, so I think he'll be fine with me taking it from here," said Hillman. The city cop shook his head. He wasn't happy but just walked off dejected.

Two other squad cars—one, state police and the other, a deputy—blocked the motel entrance, with their lights still flashing. Doc and Sal lowered their hands and Sal bent to pick up his .45.

"Sal, you better leave it there. I think this is the most action the city cops have seen in a while. You don't want to get yourself shot."

Sal stood back up, with some difficulty. "Man, I'm gonna be hurting. Took a tumble. What the fuck?" He turned and looked at his hippy van and said, "Son-of-a-bitch! The motherfuckers blew a hole in the fucking eagle. I think it was an eagle." Sure enough, the majestic bird painted on the side of his van had been decapitated by a load of buckshot. He walked around his vehicle, cussing all the way. "You were fucking lucky, Doc. There's three dents in the door but none of them went through. The cocksucker must have been using a peashooter." Doc was still shaky, and he looked at the dents and holes. In addition to the destroyed eagle, two more loads of buckshot had strafed side of the van. One at the top edge near the back and the other at the bottom, just behind the driver-side door. There were also three small caliber holes in the mural below the eagle.

While Doc and Sal surveyed the carnage, the Sheriff walked up behind them, unnoticed. "Y'all seem to be trouble magnets. You have any idea who was trying to kill you or why. You ain't got caught in a compromising position with anybody's wife, have you?" He was amused at his own attempt at humor. "You know, it's been at least a couple of years since we had any shooting on the streets of LaGrange. Last time I remember was two drunk deer hunters popping caps at one another, but they couldn't see straight enough to hit anything except by mistake."

Sally just shook his head in disgust and spit into the gravel. Doc said, "There was an old Ford truck that seemed to have an unnatural interest in us. Saw them several times and they were looking hard at us. Couple of Mexican boys . . ."

Sally broke in "Fucking wetbacks! That's what they were. If I could have got off a good shot, they'd be a couple dead fucking wetbacks." He reached down and brushed the dust off his pistol, released the slide and put it in his back pocket.

"I think there was another car that followed us—an older Chevy—from somewhere around the courthouse. I believe they both were shooting at us."

"Well, that kind of goes with what the officer told me. He said when he was headed this way, he saw two vehicles going in opposite directions, fast. But he thought he should check on the shooting," offered the Sheriff.

"Obviously, this has something to do with the girl. Nobody has any reason to fuck with us around here," said Doc and Sally nodded his head.

"Maybe obvious, maybe not. Let's go someplace where we can sit down," said Hillman. "My office is just next to the courthouse. Y'all can ride with me. I'll have somebody take some pictures of your vehicle. Maybe we can find some of the bullets or something. Leave your keys in the van for now, if you don't mind."

Doc and Sal climbed into the back seat of the Sheriff's big Suburban and they drove the four blocks to his office. Once inside, he led them to a conference room, and they took seats. "Y'all mind if I record this? My memory ain't as good as it once was." Without them answering, he pulled a tape recorder out of a drawer in a credenza against the wall and pushed the 'record' button.

"OK, now y'all tell me your life stories, but you can skip the part up to the last time I saw you."

Doc and Sal told about seeing the rusty red 150 skid off the road when they were driving to the barbeque trailer. They mentioned seeing the men from the truck on the phone at the 7-Eleven store. They said they ate their barbeque at the covered bleachers in the city park. Doc said he had seen the truck again at the truck stop café when they went out later. This brought a surprised look from Sal but he didn't speak. They told of going to the beer joint on the east edge of town and Doc added, "Your deputy, that Schaer guy, found us there and acted like we were on the run or something. Anyway, he told us some stuff about the girl. Has any report come back from Austin yet?"

"Schaer is an asshole. Why do you have somebody like that little weasel in your department?" Sal offered.

"Yeah, I know. What's a man gonna do. Bobby's my brother-in-law. That's neither here nor there. What did y'all do after that? Oh, and we won't hear anything from the state guys until tomorrow, at the earliest."

"We ain't gonna have to wait around for that, I hope!" Sal was getting pretty irritated, so Doc gave him a 'settle down' gaze.

They went on to tell of their side trip to Warda and Hillman asked, "Did you drop your empty on the floor and watch it roll away? That's about the highlight of a trip to Warda," and he laughed. Doc figured that the listing floor of that little beer joint had to be a 'must-see' highlighted in Warda's official travel brochure.

Then they told of the gunfire as they parked in their spot at the motel. That was about it. Hillman asked, "What do you guys think this is all about?"

Sal said, "Whatever it's about, now it's got personal! If I see them mojados, they are gonna be a bunch dead Mexicans."

"Hold on there! This is something for the law to sort out. You will damn sure get on my bad side if you go looking for trouble. You got that?" said Hillman.

"Bullshit! Trouble done come and found us. I ain't standing around waiting to get shot. If it goes down, it's gonna look more like the Alamo than Goliad. I'll take as many of um with me as I can. You can take that to the bank," Sally was on a roll.

"Settle down now. You have three branches of the law involved in this now and that's gonna just increase. So just keep your head down and let us handle it. It's gonna get complicated enough once the state guys get involved but it is what it is. I can't control that."

Doc wanted to bring the talk back to something that might show some progress. "Look, it is obvious that this is all about the girl—you know it as well as we do. Sally and I are both professional men with good reputations in our communities and in our respective industries. Just a couple of guys who like to get away from it all once in a while and shake the stresses from our lives. We are not the bad guys here. You know that."

There was silence for a minute, so he continued, "I've been thinking on this and I believe this is either slave trade or serious drug business—and I am not talking about some kid selling a dime bag of grass. Maybe both. From what

Schaer said, the girl had been kept prisoner. Maybe a sex prisoner. What I can't figure is why the guy in the Monte Carlo, Impala, whatever, was doing out driving her around at 5:30 in the morning. Could he have been picking her up after a sex party or something? Maybe moving her from one place to another for some reason. If that's it, she can't be the only girl involved. There have to be others suffering the same shit. Have you thought about that?"

Hillman tilted his Stetson back on his head, puffed his cheeks, and blew out a long breath. "Maybe you should be the cop in this whole thing. Yeah, we have considered all of that. Well, except for wondering why her and the guy were out and about early of a morning. That's all I'm saying about this. It's an ongoing investigation. Hasn't even started yet. Not really."

They gave their best description of the old Ford pickup. Hillman interrupted twice with demeaning comments about their ability to identify motor vehicles. The Sheriff seemed to enjoy the dialog. He said they would issue APB for the truck, but he didn't think there would be more than a few thousand like it in the immediate area. Then he drove them back to their motel.

When they arrived back at the Riverview, two state police officers were still looking over Sal's van. Sal greeted them with, "Y'all about done poking around my van? I need to see how much damage was done."

One of the patrolmen produced a paper envelope and emptied its contents into his hand so Hillman, Doc and Sal could see. They moved under the light in front of the room 29 door and the men all peered down at the three partly squashed bullets and a dozen deformed double-aught buckshot. Hillman spoke, "Looks like a .38 of some kind. Nothing too serious—just lead ball ammo, not hollow points or high velocity bullets. The others are obvious. Somebody was out to kill you boys. Or scare the shit out of you." He looked from Sal to Doc.

"Scaring somebody don't include shooting at you and fucking up a man's classic ride. Do you think? Maybe popping off a round over your head or using especially offensive language would be for scaring somebody off," said Sal. Some officers snickered and others just smiled.

"Well, I have to agree that they were after more than chasing y'all off. And it's a damn shame about your 'classic ride'," said Hillman.

"You damn right! Look at my van. You can't fix holes like that with a little Bondo, and that painting was one-of-a-kind! There ain't no replacing that. Who's gonna pay for my damages? And, I may have internal injuries from getting knocked out on the ground. What are you gonna do about that?"

Doc just looked at his feet and shook his head. He knew there was no stopping his friend now. He didn't even try.

One of the state cops said, "Just settle down now, mister. You need to be happy you weren't hurt bad or killed. Nothing else really matters, does it?"

"You're goddamn right it matters! You can't fix some shit, and this is some of that shit. I just hope I get my hands on the no-dick sons-a-bitches . . ." and his rath just sort of trailed off as he looked up at the Texas sky. He walked to the double doors on the passenger side of the van, opened them and sat down on edge of the filthy blue shag, shaking his head.

"OK, what's our next step? Are we supposed to stay or go? What do you want us to do?" Doc asked.

"I'm gonna put a deputy on the motel for tonight in case anybody comes back with evil intentions. Let's circle back up in the morning. By then, we might have something back from Austin about the girl. You suppose y'all can go and lock yourselves in your room and stay out of trouble until then?" said Hillman.

"We can do that."

"Good. You know, it was just lucky for me that I was even downtown tonight—or maybe, unlucky. I am president of the Leopard Booster Club, and we had a meeting at the library tonight. You know, football season will be here before you know it. Anyway, my wife is probably worried sick, so I need to get home. Damn, it's after midnight. Hell of a day. Y'all be good!" and the Sheriff turned and walked back to his Suburban. The other cops drifted in different directions, except the deputy stuck with babysitting the motel for the night.

***

It took a little prodding, but Doc finally convinced Sal to close up the van and come into their room. Inside, Sal just sat on his bed with a thousand-yard stare, while Doc brushed his teeth and put on Seger concert shirt to sleep in. When he walked back from the bathroom, Sal was still just sitting.

"Man, it don't do you no good to get so worked up. I know this was a truly fucked-up day—and night. But, hell, we still got our youth and good looks! What more can a couple of fifty-year-olds want?" and he patted Sal on the shoulder and sat down on his own bed, across from his friend.

Finally, Sal looked up and half-smiled. "You have always been a defender of women. I think you are set on finding out what happened to that poor girl and any more like her. I'm with you, brother. You know, when I got home from the war, I thought I was done with putting myself in harm's way but I just keep on doing it. And it's usually when I'm around you. I hope you don't get us killed."

"Me too," was all that Doc said. He knew Sal was

right about his always seeming to be in the defense of the defenseless—but not just limited to women. He knew most women were strong and could take care of themselves. But he had also known women who had been mistreated or were preyed upon by evil men.

His empathy stimmed from his relationship with his mother, who was vulnerable after his father's death. He had been her defender throughout her valiant fight against cancer until it finally took her from him. He had fought several battles for his second wife, Kay—a strong, beautiful, passionate, and difficult woman who brought most of her troubles on herself—but his love had been stronger than any thought for his own safety. He and Sally had been behind retribution for a young woman who had been raped, beaten, and trampled upon by the legal system, back during their biker days. Doc had continued to champion the advancement of women and minorities in his professional life. Nothing was more despicable to him than the those who prey upon the powerless. In his mind, this didn't make him noble—only human.

The other side of Doc's attitude about women was that he knew they were all crazy. He knew it and made peace with it, while still in his teens. He had given up on understanding women. It was hopeless. He thought that no man could understand them. Any man who thought he could was probably crazy himself. But he loved them as a species. Peculiar, exotic, beautiful, unattainable animals to be appreciated but never to be controlled and certainly never to be owned.

That night, Doc dreamed of himself at twenty-five, with Kay behind him on his Harley—just riding on an empty, tree-lined country road to nowhere. Sleep often found Doc on that road. Sal didn't dream. He taught himself not to after years of night sweats and waking, finding himself still in Vietnam. Some things can be left behind. Some cannot.

***

4.

Doc thought it looked like rain out the window of room 29 on Saturday morning. He could hear thunder to the west, across the Colorado. He felt restless, like there was something he should be doing. Sal was still asleep. Doc didn't have to wait long because, as he turned from the window, there was a knock on the door. Still cautious, he peeked through the curtain and saw Major Naiser and Sheriff Hillman standing outside.

He cracked the door and could hear Sal moving, awake now. "Mighty early in the morning for a couple of notable officers of the constabulary to be knocking on my door," said Doc.

Naiser spoke, "Yeah, well sorry about that. I need you boys to get up and meet us over at the sheriff's office. Take your time but be there in a half-hour, if you don't mind." And they turned and walked away with no further explanation.

Doc looked back and said, "Get your lard ass out of bed! We gotta get to the sheriff's office ASAP. I think the Sheriff and Naiser always look like they are in a pissing contest. I don't think they like one another very much."

Sal was trying to sit up and clear his head. "Ain't that how it's supposed to be. Marking their territory."

"I'll run and get us some coffee and kolaches while you get your shit together," said Doc. He dressed in yesterday's jeans and shirt, grabbed the van's keys and drove to the truck stop café just down the street. He was back in ten minutes with paper cups of weak coffee and good apricot and cottage cheese kolaches. Sal was up and dressed, in his only extra set of overalls, since the ones he had on last night had lost the strap button.

They inhaled their breakfast and climbed into the van with Sal driving this time. "Man, I wish you would look at how them bastards fucked up my damn van. Holes everywhere! Son-of-a-bitch!"

"Well brother, on the bright side, since you're too damn cheap to get the air conditioner fixed, we can use the extra ventilation."

"Yeah, well fuck you, Doc!" and they both laughed.

They walked into the sheriff's office and a deputy told them to go to the same room where they had spoken the night before. At the table were Naiser, Hillman and two other men they did not recognize. None of them looked too comfortable with each other—or with their Saturday being interrupted. Hillman said, "Sit down, boys. We have some interesting stuff to talk about. The gentleman in the suit is with the Attorney General's office. His name is James Ryley. The other man is a Texas Ranger, name of William Stafford." The men nodded at Doc and Sal without reaching out to shake hands.

Ryley spoke, "I'm just sort of here to get an idea what's going on. Should be floating the Comal with my kids today, so you'll excuse me if my mood isn't too good." The man seemed out of place, but he said it with an earnest smile. Then, "We may bring the Rangers in on this so Will is going to be working with Sheriff Hillman, for now, at least, until we get this thing sorted out a bit." The Ranger just nodded and fingered the brim of his hat, which lay crown-down on the table. Hillman looked even more uncomfortable.

"OK, so what do you need out of us? Why don't you let us go on our way? You know, we had sort of a get-away planned and it didn't involve laying around at the damn Riverview Motel." said Sal.

Naiser responded, "Well, that might have been

possible except for the unpleasant business last night. You're not exactly in protective custody but we want you around here for at least today to see where this is all going to lead."

Sal shuffled around in his chair and gave Doc a disapproving look. Doc just shook his head.

Hillman said, "We have some information we probably shouldn't share with you, but this is not a normal situation. And we appreciate all you boys are going through. I'll let John fill us all in."

"Thanks, Sheriff. Early this morning we found two burned out vehicles in the area. One was a '77 Ford 150 pickup, red in color, but that had been painted over decades ago—originally, it was white. We found that one on a ranch road off of Highway 71 south of here. The other one was a 1989 Chevrolet Caprice. Gray. It was reported on fire by a local farmer in the parking lot of a Catholic church at the little crossroads called Holman. That's south of here, as well. The two sites were about nine miles apart. We think they were the two vehicles involved in the assault on you men last night. We may need you to take a look at them to be sure. We will let you know about that. Might not be able to tell, anyway. They were burned up pretty badly. Interestingly, both vehicles are shown to be stolen—years ago—and they had stolen and altered license plates on them. This ain't something we see every day."

Doc listened and said, "Don't y'all think this kind of stuff indicates something bigger? I mean, dead girl, shooting at us, mystery vehicles—burned to hide something. There's a hell of a lot more to this than some runaway chick having a tiff with her boyfriend or something."

"The direction of our investigation isn't something you need to be worried about. We will let you know when we need your input. About the girl, the autopsy just came in before you fellows got here. We were studying it when you walked in. Why don't y'all step out in the hall while we finish digesting the Fax. Get you a cup of coffee or something. I think there's kolaches or donuts or something in the break room down the hall," said Naiser. Hillman opened the door and pointed them toward the kitchen.

Walking toward the break room, Sal said, "Brother, I think you are right about this whole thing. I've been considering it all, but you are ahead of me getting it sorted out."

"Don't know about all that. I want to hear what they say about the girl." They rounded the corner and spotted the coffee maker and what was left of a box of pastries.

"I can always put away a few more of these things!" said Sal as he attacked the box. "Assholes! They ate all the good ones. Nothing but some limp dick strawberry kolaches and a apple fritter left. Shit."

Doc poured coffee into one of the heavy mugs emblazoned with a picture of a Fayette County Sheriff's badge. He added cream and blue bag, stirred it with a plastic straw and sipped. "You gotta try some of this coffee. Beats the hell out of the truck stop swill."

Sal's cheeks were bulging with apple fritter as he poured himself a cup—black and they sat down on the folding chairs. Doc looked hard at one of the strawberry pastries but put it back in the box. Just as they were getting comfortable, Ryley tapped on the door frame and said, "I think they are ready for you now." And walking down the hall he asked, "Quinn, what do you do for a living? You look familiar to me."

"You can call me Doc. Everybody does. Anyway, I am vice president of operations for Talmadge Oilfield Services. My office is in San Antonio." Doc thought formal to formal was appropriate, though he seldom gave out his title. He took an immediate dislike for the man. Ryley seemed to him to be a politician, pure and simple. Not somebody who would be involved in an investigation. And a lawyer, on top of it all. Doc had a distaste for most lawyers.

"Yeah, I think you appeared before the Railroad Commission a while back. That's where I know you from. I'm not a commissioner but was an interested spectator at the meeting."

"Yeah, probably. Those affairs are a lot like being on trial, sometimes," Doc said, and Ryley laughed.

They all sat back down at the conference table and Sal asked, "OK, what can you tell us about the girl? Doc here has been losing sleep worrying about it and he can be a real pussy when he's upset."

"Asshole," said Doc, out of the side of his mouth.

Naiser spoke, "This was a young woman who had known lots of misery. She was just a kid—sixteen or seventeen." What he didn't say was that the State medical examiner believed she was probably from Mexico, based on the kind of dental work she had in her mouth. She had been sexually active, apparently for a few years and had been treated very roughly and probably even abused with what the examiner called 'foreign objects.' She had been burned with cigarettes or cigars or something else on her upper back, arms, and buttocks but the examiner said the scars were at least several months old. All Naiser said was, "She had been abused and had burn scars, but you don't need to know more than that." He turned the first Fax sheet and gazed at second.

Doc was shaking his head, eyes down. "Who does this kind of shit? I've known some terrible people in my lifetime but not even the worst of them would do something like that to a kid. I hope."

Naiser looked up from the Fax and said, "Well, maybe something on this report will give you some idea of what we are dealing with. She may have been a drug addict. Those details are still being investigated." Again, Naiser didn't reveal all the report detailed. She had been injecting—or was being injected with something, for an extended period. She had one broken needle in her arm and a couple of her veins had collapsed. She was evidently being given shots between her toes. Probably heroin but it was impossible to know for sure until the tox screen was completed and that would take several days due to a backlog in Austin.

Naiser did say, "There was residue on her dress and on the soles of her shoes that's being analyzed now. They did test that and the stuff on her huaraches was easy to test—brown Mexican heroin."

"So, what does that mean? Was she a sex slave they kept strung out on junk or something else," Sal asked.

"We can't speak to that. The investigation has just started. We can share some general information but nothing specific." said the Ranger, speaking for the first time. "We know how that kind of thing usually operates. We have seen how they get the heroin ready for selling. Usually in a closed room someplace where they can cut down the purity and bag it up in either little glassine bags or balloons for street sales or something bigger for bulk transactions. Anyway, the people doing the work are usually women and they make them work naked so they can't steal anything. Hell, you can get that kind of information in the newspaper or on TV." What *he* didn't say was what they do with the women when they are not processing heroin. It was anybody's guess. Maybe get them addicted and use them for sex or prostitute them. Or maybe they just held them for gang use only.

"Sir, I appreciate what you are telling us, but where do we fit into all this? We are basically just a couple of pain-in-the-ass innocent bystanders," said Sal, acknowledging the respect due to a Texas Ranger.

"No, after last night, you are more than that. Maybe you and that hideous thing you ride around in are bait. The bad guys know you are the only ones who could have possibly seen the girl go off the cliff and the car she rode up in. I'm sure they have no idea how incompetent you were at identifying that car."

"You might want to lighten up! It was fucking dark that morning and we were just finishing our damn breakfast. We didn't have any idea some sort of malfeasance was about to take place," was Sal's retort.

Hillman spoke, "I think that's about all we can tell you right now. Y'all can go on back to the Riverview or just hang around town if you want to. I would recommend that you let my office know if you plan to run off to any exotic spots like Warda again. If you do, maybe we can trail you with a deputy."

"Honest to God! Do you have any idea how long this is going to go on?" Sal demanded.

"Long as it takes. You boys might want to let your family and place of business know you might not be in on Monday. I hope we are done by then, but I wouldn't bet on it." Naiser and Ranger Stafford nodded their agreement.

"God Damn!! Some fucked up vacation this is turning out to be," bellowed Sal.

"Well, just think about the story you will have to tell your grandchildren," said Naiser and the other officers were laughing as Doc and Sal made their retreat.

When they were our of earshot, Hillman said to the others, "Look, I know you state folks are going to take a role in this investigation—and I appreciate it on some level—but we don't need to be tripping all over each other here. This thing involves my county and I'm going to need to be involved. The people who elected me expect that. If the state police, the Rangers and whoever else from Austin makes a move, I expect to be kept in the loop. Can we agree on that?"

Ryley chuckled and shook his head. "Sheriff, we will involve you as much as you need to be involved but this may be too big for your department. Especially if it goes beyond this damn girl falling off a cliff."

"Unless you see something that goes beyond the county line, you need to remember what your limits are. That's my last word for now," said Sheriff Hillman. The men all went their own ways, each thinking the ball was in his court.

***

5.

"Well, we seem stuck here again. What do you want to do to kill some time. Ain't like LaGrange is the center of the excitement universe. This is gonna bore me shitless—specially if I can't just stay stoned and rubbing up against some cherubesque dumplin'," Sal said as he drove his wounded van from the cop shop.

Doc remained silent.

"If you want to, we can go hunting for some companionship. There's gotta be some action someplace around here. You need to get your pipes cleaned out, Doc!"

Still no reply from Doc.

As he pulled into the motel lot and stopped in front of room 29, Sal looked over at his friend and stared for a moment and said, "OK brother, you got something on your mind. What the hell are you so deep in thought about?"

After a beat, Doc opened the glove box and extracted the Rand McNally and said, "Been thinking about this whole pile of shit. I want to look at the map and find out if I'm just imagining things or maybe . . ." and he opened his door and they walked into their room. Doc spread the map book out on the little round table by their window and turned on the light hanging above it, with Sal leaning over his shoulder. He knew Doc's wheels were turning. He'd seen it before. The book had Texas broken into four pages. LaGrange was in the northwest part of the southeast page. He flipped to the pages showing the northern sections and back and forth.

"Hand me that note pad and the pen by the phone." and Sal complied. Doc began scribbling notes on the pad,

Sal still uncertain of his direction.

When he got tired of wondering, Sal asked, "What in the hell are you trying to figure out?"

Doc looked up at Sal and said, "Look at this. We are located in a prime area to go anywhere in Texas—well, maybe anywhere except the Panhandle or El Paso. LaGrange is right where you might want to be to have easy access to I-10 and I-35 and most of 71 is 4-lane now. Straight shot to heavy traffic areas going to Houston, San Antonio, Austin, and Dallas. Highway 71 might be a key route. Look!"

Sal studied the map and flipped the pages. "Yeah, so? What's that supposed to tell us?"

"From right here in 'Hootersville' you can make it to the biggest markets in the state. I know something about location for marketing purposes. Presuming you had a way to get the junk to this area, then you could distribute to 90% of the state's market along perfect routes. Good road with lower traffic with access to major Interstate highways." They silently studied the map for several minutes.

Finally, Sal said, "You need to learn how to fuckin' write. I can't read a word you put on that pad."

"Oh, go to hell! I'm no damn draftsman. I'll read it to you. Clean your fucking glasses."

They talked for an hour about dope dealers and highways and what to do with their day. Back in their biker days—in the 1970s—they had learned a lot about how an outlaw club conducted its commerce. That club, the Devil's Jokers, controlled not only the motorcycle club scene for three states but also prostitution and drugs. They used the Interstate Highway system to their advantage and knew how to camouflage their movements. And who to pay off to cover their tracks. Doc and Sal figured some of that strategy was still workable, even more than twenty years later.

But a lot of things had changed in those years. Drugs—hard drugs—had ceased being a friendly business. Maybe it never had been. Heroin had spread from the limited community of blacks and outlaws to become a drug of choice for hipsters of all stripes, including considerable numbers of the middle and affluent classes. The influx of Mexican brown dope had made it easier and cheaper to find than the China white of the earlier era. AIDS had become a scourge among the gay population and with idiots who used dirty needles to inject heroin and other drugs.

The Feds were fighting the Drug War on several fronts—cocaine, heroin, meth, pot—but their efforts seemed to be concentrated on the borders and in the major cities. Probably not so much in rural, Central Texas. That might be an oversight and the fact wasn't lost on Doc and Sal. "Sally, after thinking about it, I wonder why there were only state and local guys in that little meeting today. I mean, they had identified smack as being involved. Shouldn't that be something DEA or somebody would be interested in?" mused Doc.

"Hell man, I don't know. This shit is getting too deep for me. I suppose they are all jealous of their territory. Let's go for a ride."

"Hey, take a look at this." Doc pointed to tiny print on the map—Holman. "Let's take a ride down 71 and then mosey over to that church. Maybe the burned-out car is still there. They said the truck was on a ranch road off of 71. Nine miles from the church. I bet we can find it, if it hasn't been hauled away. Just curious."

"Beats the shit out of sitting around here. Let's go!"

***

Highway 71 had once been a narrow 2-lane but had

been rebuilt as a wide, well-traveled artery from Columbus on I-10 to Austin, on I-35 and points north. Sal drove as Doc studied the Rand McNally. He had marked the location of St. Wenceslaus Catholic Church at Homan but, it was only after they were several miles from LaGrange that he noticed something he should have considered earlier. "Hey man, you can't get to Homan from here! There are no bridges across the river between LaGrange and Columbus." The Texas Colorado River is not as mighty as its western cousin of the same name, but it still has limited crossing points, especially in sparsely populated regions.

"Well, that do present a problem, now don't it. So, if the two vehicles got burned up by the same bunch, they must have had a pretty good idea what they were doing."

"Well, what it tells me is that all roads lead back through LaGrange, one way or another. Maybe leaving the truck and car south of town was to mislead somebody. What do you think?" asked Doc.

"Seems logical to me, but then I ain't no cop and I'm not any kind of expert about this part of the country. Might be something we ask Hillman about."

Continuing down Hwy. 71, just south of the community of Ellinger, they saw a flat-bed wrecker pulling onto the highway. On its bed was the sagging hulk of what had once been a Ford 150. "Well, we almost made it in time. Let's see if we can find the place where it was burned," said Doc.

Sal turned down the gravel road where the wrecker had been. They only had to drive about a quarter-mile before finding a row of scorched cedars and a black patch on the side of the road. Recent rains had things damp enough that it didn't cause a prairie fire. They got out of the van and walked over to the burned ground but there was nothing to see so they climbed back in and retraced the route back to 71. They would have to go back to LaGrange to get to Homan.

As they drove north past Ellinger, Doc noticed an unmarked, light blue Ford Crown Vic with a spotlight mounted driver-side door. It was parked in the lot of a little store—facing the highway. Behind the wheel and crouched down was a narrow-shouldered man with a ballcap, pulled down tight. "Did you see that?"

"Fuckin' A. That worm, Schaer. Must have been trailing us since we left the motel."

"For our own protection, no doubt. He wasn't even in uniform."

"A hell of a lot of protection he'd be. Let's just keep going and see if he stays on us. I'll stop at the first gas station in LaGrange and see what he does."

When they pulled in at a Texaco station, the blue Ford drove past, without slowing. It parked at the truck stop café, still in full view. Schaer didn't get out of his car but just swung it in a loop, aiming back toward the street.

"Wanna fuck with him?" asked Sal with an evil grin.

"Nah, let's don't give the little bastard the satisfaction. I just wonder if Hillman put him up to this or if he's freelancing. He must know that we know he's following us. He can't be that dumb. Can he?"

"I try to never underestimate the stupidity of assholes."

"Let's try that Mexican joint out past the courthouse square. My kolaches are wearing off," said Doc. The idea of lunch always appealed to Fat Sally.

They drove, in city traffic, to La Hacienda Bonita and parked behind the building. Deputy Schaer followed, two cars back, still trying to be stealthy, and parked on the curb a block away.

The place was busy for a Saturday lunchtime but the lady behind the register pointed them to a table in one corner of the room. As they strolled over, Sal said,

"Whoever named this dump 'Bonita' had a good imagination. Or a sense of humor."

"Maybe the food is better than décor," Doc said, and they both eyed the plates in front of their fellow diners. That always helps a man decide what to order.

A slim, young Hispanic woman delivered chips and salsa and took their orders. As she walked away, Sal said, "Now, that's more like it. That, my brother, is damn sure *bonita*."

Doc just nodded and smiled his approval. The chips were out of a bag and the salsa was thin and vinegary, but their enchilada combo plates were actually above average and the big plastic tumblers of tea nicely washed it all down.

When they walked back to Sal's van, there were four locals—looked like cowboys—eyeing the van. "Howdy, guys. How can we help you?" asked Sal.

The oldest cowboy—a man looking to be around 60—answered, "What in the world happened to your truck? Looks like somebody wasn't too fond of hippies." All of the men were laughing.

"Well now, I guess that's a fact," replied Sal. "We sure as hell ain't no hippies but some men copped an attitude about us last night. We was just innocent bystanders and they started popping caps on us."

Another of the cowboys said, "Damn shame. Got any idea who done the shooting?"

Doc said, "We're working on that. Hey, can y'all tell us the best way to a place called Holman? I think it's someplace south of here."

"Ain't really no town. Just a big old Catholic church there. You looking for somebody in particular?" said the old cowboy.

"Not really," said Sal. And the cowboys looked at one another and older one gave some general directions and the four walked off toward the door to the restaurant.

"Let's go take a look," said Doc and they climbed into Sal's recently ventilated van and went to search for a burned-out car. The route wasn't straight, and the directions were sketchy, so it took over a half-hour for them to locate St. Wenceslaus. The church was visible from several miles away, once they were in the area. When they arrived, there was a Sheriff's Department cruiser with a deputy behind the wheel, guarding the site. They had seen him before—with Schaer at the beer joint the night before. When Sal pulled the van to a stop, the young Hispanic deputy got out of the air-conditioned comfort of his car and held his hand up for the van to stop.

"Good morning, gents! Well, I guess it's afternoon. I'm not surprised to see you out here. Saw you last night at Starter's—that's the lounge where Deputy Schaer found y'all last night. I'm Johnny Lopez. We didn't get introduced then." He seemed like a friendly type, open to conversation as he leaned against his squad car.

"Good day to you," said Doc. "We were just wondering about the car you are guarding here. You know, we got shot up after we saw you last night."

"Yeah. Hell, everybody in town knows about that by now. Close call, I hear. Sure left some impressive holes in your ride!"

Sal spoke, "It's a damn shame. Fucking up a classic like this," as he pointed to the mark that took the head off his eagle—or, at least, he always thought it was an eagle. "We thought we'd take a look at this burned up car to see if we recognized it from the shooting."

"Can't imagine it would have been nothin' else. You can look all you want."

The car was almost unidentifiable as to model, but the chrome insignia of a Caprice Classic was on the gravel lot at the rear of the hulk. The interior was entirely gone and the trunk lid stood straight up, warped from the explosion of the gas tank. The tires had burned and the whole mess squatted low in the sunshine. Everyone knew there was no real evidence to be found. All three of them walked circles around it. There was what looked like a bullet hole, low in the rear, driver-side door.

Doc pointed to it and Sal said, "Looks like a .45 to me. I guess I actually hit something." He was proud.

The three walked back to the Lopez cruiser and leaned against it. Doc lit a Marlboro and offered one to the deputy, who accepted it and asked for a light. "You know, since yesterday morning we have been a world of shit here in Fayette County. Is it usually like this around here. Fucking wild west!"

The deputy laughed and said, "No, man! Nothing ever happens around here. At least not like this shit. You guys gave the whole town something to buzz about."

"Hey, if your Sheriff would have let us go on our way after we saw that chick jump yesterday, we would have been out of your hair. There wouldn't have been no gunfire on the streets of LaGrange last night. Hell, me and Doc would probably be enjoying the company of some sweet things and forgetting we ever heard of LaGrange."

That gave Lopez a good laugh as he removed his glasses and cleaned the lenses on his handkerchief. "That's probably true. But, hey! That was awful about that girl. Probably just some poor *chica* who didn't deserve what she got. What I understand is she was pretty mistreated. Maybe some sort of sex slave or something? Do y'all know any more about her? I know you were meeting with the Sheriff and some guys from the state police."

"What you said is about all we know. Is there a history of drug running or maybe human smuggling going on around here?" asked Doc.

"Man, they feed me just enough information to do

my job. I keep my head down and don't ask too many questions. You know, I'm second generation Mexican with the Sheriff's Department. My father was the first deputy of our kind for as long as anybody could remember. It's a good job and I like it, so I just do what they ask me to. I'd like to be a Highway Patrol officer. I'd need to go to the academy for that, but that's my plan. There are lots of us in the State Police these days. I got a cousin with them."

"What can you tell us about Deputy Schaer?" Sal wanted to know.

Lopez rolled his eyes but then thought better of that gesture and put his mirrored aviator glasses back on. "He's sort of the head deputy, I guess. Not nothing formal. I mean, no title or nothing. He's Sheriff Hillman's brother-in-law. I think that's about all there is to tell."

"Why haven't they picked up this pile of shit yet? We went by where the truck was burned and a wrecker had winched the carcass up on the flat bed and hauled it off," asked Doc.

"They are supposed to do that. I'm just waiting around until the wrecker gets here. I think we only have one of them rollback flatbed trucks in town. Driver's probably at lunch after hauling the pickup off. I can get on the radio and check if you want me to."

"Naw man. That won't be necessary. We are just being nosy. You know, this whole thing has kinda fucked up our little getaway. Hey, thanks for the information," said Sal.

"Thanks for the smoke. Sheriff don't like me smoking in the squad car."

***

"Well, what now? Looking at burnt up grease spots and scrap metal hasn't told us a hell of a lot," Sal said as they drove back toward LaGrange.

"Hell, I don't know. If I had a better idea what to look for, maybe we could come up with some ideas. Just being would-be detectives is kind of useless. Just a thought! Why don't we ride back up to Monument Hill. It's nice there. Breezy and shady and peaceful. Always loved that place."

"Yeah, I know. You want your fucking ashes blowing back in your loved ones faces up there. Probably my face too—nah, you'll outlive my lard ass."

Doc reached into the cooler behind his captain's chair and pulled out two Lone Stars. "We gotta stop for beer and ice. These just been resting in cool water and they're the last two."

The route they had followed to get to the church involved turns down several country roads and Sal made a wrong turn onto a rough stretch of sand and gravel—mostly sand—which dead-ended at the edge of a barely flowing little creek. "This ain't the way we came," he said and began backing up to find a place to turn around.

"You think?" was Doc's reply. Then he asked, "You seen anything of our shadow on this little excursion."

"No. Maybe the little shit lost interest or just got lost. Good riddance, but I would have loved to fuck with him a little bit. Hell I couldn't have even followed myself to where we are . . . wherever we are."

Sal continued to make guesses on how to get back to town and the Rand McNally was of no use on these uncharted roads. The route he chose took them several miles farther to the west into an area with more trees and less people. Up ahead they could see what appeared to be a more substantial road. They were just passing a long gravel drive led back to a large metal building with several vehicles parked outside. One of them was a maroon

Corvette.

"Slow down, Sally!"

"What? We are almost back to civilization now. I think." But he slowed almost to a stop.

"Back up a little. I think I just saw the 'Vette that was at the honkytonk last night." Sal backed the van up enough to get a good look down the driveway to the building.

"Yeah, that looks like it. That's one of them 40th anniversary models, I think. A '93. So what?"

"Nothing. Just wondering what a dapper dresser driving that car would be doing out here in the boonies. Probably nothing. Let's go."

As they drove away, a heavyset Mexican man carrying a shotgun walked around the side of the building and stared at the back of the retreating van. They didn't see him.

It took another half-hour for them to reach anything approaching real 'civilization' and when they pulled back onto Hwy. 71, they were ten miles west of LaGrange.

"Yeah Sal, you have a real feel for this driving thing, don't you. Where the hell did you take us?"

"Bullshit! You were supposed to be navigating."

They eventually crossed the northern bridge and stopped at the same 7-Eleven store where they had seen the red truck using the pay phone the day before. They drained the Coleman and stocked it with fresh ice and a case of Lone Star and drove on back up to Monument Hill. It was crowded. It was Saturday afternoon and there were families and old people walking along the paths from the monuments to the old brewery location on the lip of the hill. A different park ranger was on duty—they didn't see Ranger Stamper—but the lady who was worried that her magazines be properly returned was at the information desk. They saw her through the window as they pulled to a stop in an empty space. Sal chugged the last of his beer before they got out.

"You know, brother, this is a pretty cool place. I mean, with or without the martyred patriots of Texas. Just a damn nice place. Maybe it's not such a bad place to toss you after you're done using your dilapidated old body."

"As long as the wind is in the right direction," said Doc. They walked the paths and again went to the place where the young woman had leaped. The crime tape was long gone and there was no sign of this modern martyr and most in the crowd, being from Houston and Dallas and San Antonio and elsewhere, had no idea. They sat on the same bench where they had their breakfast thirty-six hours earlier. Each man was wondering if it could have actually been only a day-and-a-half of their lives. It seemed like so much longer. On the way back to the parking lot, they stopped to exchange pleasantries with the lady giving information.

She looked up as they walked into the cool of the office. "Well, I see you boys made it back. I'm surprised y'all are still around."

"No more than we are," said Sally. "We were asked to hang around a while."

"Seems I heard something about some shooting involving you two. Nobody got hurt, I hope."

"No ma'am. Just my ride," said Sal. "Is there anything fun to do around here on a Saturday night?"

"I reckon that depends on what you call fun. Let me see . . . Oh! There's a dance at the SPJST Hall in Fayetteville tonight. It ain't far. There's a group called Asleep at the Wheel supposed to play. I think they do stuff like Bob Wills and the Texas Playboys. Y'all might like that. There'll be a crowd, I'm sure."

"Yeah! I have seen them before. When they played in San Antone a couple of years back. What do you think,

Sally? Could be fun."

"Ma'am, are there usually some . . . uh . . . unattached ladies at them dances?" Sal wanted to know.

"Well, you just never know, now do you?" said the woman and she jiggled all over when she laughed. "You do know how to polka and two-step, don't you."

Sal was right there. "Lady, there ain't no dance I can't do!" and they all laughed. For all his size and bluster, there were few who could match Sal on the dance floor.

As they walked out, both men thanked the lady for the suggestion. Just as they reached the van, a maroon Corvette screamed down the road in front of the lot, slammed on breaks to make the sharp left turn and gunned the engine. Doc stopped in his tracks and walked over to the Park Ranger, who was depositing some sandwich bags and empty pop bottles in a big yellow garbage can.

"Yes sir, can I help you?" asked the Ranger.

"Yes sir, if you can. Do you know who drives that maroon-colored Corvette? They guy just drove by like a bat out of hell. Not too safe."

The Ranger looked toward the road and shook his head. "Far as I know, there's only one like that around here and he lives about a mile down the road in the biggest house on this hill. His name is Jack Darling, if you can believe that."

"We been seeing him around and I was just wondering what he does for a living. I mean, he dresses nice and drives a fine automobile. Saw him last night at a beer joint on the east side of town."

"I'm not sure. I know he's some sort of big shot. Moved here a few years ago. I think he brought money with him. Must be nice, but I wouldn't know."

"Me neither, pardner. Me neither. Thanks," said Doc and he walked back to the van with the Ranger's eyes following him all the way.

"What was that all about?"

"Nothing. I have always been curious about fat cats and how they live their lives, I guess."

"Well, I know where the 'fat cat' thing comes from. Kay had her fat cats when you met her. But, hey, she got over them when she fell in love with you. And now you are a fat cat, of sorts, yourself. Admit it!"

"Bullshit. I am not now nor will ever be any kind of fat cat. I think we are always what we start out as. You're always gonna be that little fat kid who had to kick ass to get respect and I'm always gonna be a guy who wanted to play football but wasn't good enough. We might act like something else and even make ourselves look like something else, but we are always gonna be what we always were. In our own minds, anyway."

"Shit, Doc! I hate it when you get all philosophical. Let's get cleaned up and go find us some little round-ass Bohemian girls at the dance tonight. I'll even put on my blue jeans. Least, I think I brought a pair."

***

6.

They knew that dance halls like the SPJST would have set-ups and beer, but they were thinking something else might be more to their taste on this night. They stopped at the local liquor store and picked up a bottle of Jack Daniel's Old No. 7 and headed for Fayetteville. It was about fifteen miles east of LaGrange and maybe out of the Sheriff's comfort zone for their travel, but they didn't care. It didn't take long to find the hall. Just a drive through the planned quaintness of the little Czech community and there it was.

The lot was already packed full with pickup trucks, SUVs, newer but less inexpensive Chevrolets with basic trim—what seemed to be the 'national vehicle' of the local Czech population—and a smattering of Mercedes, favored by a few of the more affluent German citizens. And one maroon Corvette. Sal parked along the road in a line that was getting longer by the minute.

"Looks like your prime suspect is here," Sal said with a chuckle as they walked past the Vette. He thought Doc's attempt at detective work was a waste of time in addition to being silly. Too many TV shows and crime novels.

That got the expected, "Fuck you," in Doc's deadpan response.

Johnny Lopez was moonlighting as crowd control in the parking lot. When he saw them, he walked toward Doc and Sal as they zig-zagged through cars toward the big, wooden hall. He waved a greeting. "I see y'all found something to do for the night. This ought to be a good party."

"Sure hope so! Hanging around Fayette County

wasn't what we planned but we'll make do with whatever comes along," said Sal. Deputy Lopez followed the boys toward the steps to the hall.

Doc asked, "Did they pick up the Chevy?"

"Hell, man! I hung around until after four, when the wrecker finally got there. What a mess!"

"Hey, we passed by a big metal building next to a tree line, what I think was northwest of the church. Several miles away—my driver didn't know where he was going. Anyway, you know what I'm talking about? Mr. Darling's Corvette was parked there with several more vehicles."

"I may know the place you're talking about. I think Darling is starting some kind of shooting club. You know, blasting away at clay birds and, maybe, doing some dove hunting. Dove season starts up in less than two weeks around here. Never seen much fun in that kind of things but some folks do, I suppose."

"OK, thanks. Just curious," said Doc as Sal gave a little shake of his head.

"You boys enjoy the party. I hear that Asleep at the Wheel ain't bad. They even got and accordion, stand-up bass, and fiddles, kinda like a Conjunto band. Otta be good." Lopez waved as he walked away and Doc and Sal moved through the group on the front porch of the hall, paid their cover charge—$5 'Stag or Drag' the sign said—and looked inside.

The room was larger than it seemed from the outside. There was a low stage at the far end of a long expanse of dance floor, polished smooth by generations of boots and high heels. On both sides of the room, folding chairs and tables were clustered with more nearer the entrance. All of the tables seemed to be filled with happy people. There was a row of beer coolers and a long table serving as a bar in one corner. There was a line of people waiting to buy beer and Cokes and little tubs of ice with red plastic cups. They scanned the room for any empty table but saw none.

"I guess we will just stand around with our thumbs up our ass," said Sal.

"Let's get in line and buy some Cokes and ice and make us a drink. There's some benches along the back wall where we might squeeze out a seat," said Doc, so they joined the line to the bar. The music hadn't started yet but the band was setting up on the little stage. They still had a half-dozen ahead of them in the line when Doc felt a tap on his shoulder. He turned and looked down into the smiling face of Jack Darling.

"Good evening, fellas! I've seen y'all around the past couple of days. When you get your set-ups, we'd be pleased if you join us at our table," and he pointed to a 6-spot table toward the front of the room.

"Well, thank you sir. My name is Connor Quinn, and this is Sal Lombardo. You can call me Doc." Darling smiled and nodded.

"Just come on over when you get served," said Darling and he walked back through the crowd, toward the far end of the room.

"Well, how 'bout that shit?" Said Sal. "Maybe he's just trying to gain your trust so you don't bring down his little human smuggling, smack sellin' empire." And he laughed at his friend, who was still staring at Darling's back.

"Shut the fuck up and get us some Cokes and ice," and Doc walked off, following Jack Darling.

When they reached Darling's table, he said, "Doc, this is my wife, Darlene and these folks are State Representative, Steve McDole, and his wife Anna. Folks, this is Connor Quinn. He's one of the guys who have been causing so much excitement around LaGrange for the past couple of days." And he laughed.

"Pleased to meet y'all. Sal Lombardo will be joining

us if he ever gets us some setups." Then, looking at Mrs. Darling, "Darlene Darling! That's quite a name," and everyone at the table laughed.

She looked down, with a mild blush, "Yes, sounds fake, doesn't it?" Darlene appeared to be in her mid-thirties, with long, very blond hair and a beautiful tan, setting off her intensely blue eyes. She wore a matching blue dress. She had a diamond pendant around her neck and a blue sapphire and diamond ring on her right hand and a four-carat engagement ring and wide platinum band on her left. Doc thought she belonged on Fifth Avenue or Rodeo Drive instead of an SPJST hall in Central Texas.

"We had another couple joining us, but they had to cancel at the last minute, so sit and let's get to know one another," said Darling, and Doc took his chair. The two wives were engaged in small talk when Doc arrived, so they continued, although the noise level in the hall was making conversation increasingly problematic. Their heads were close together and their eyes darted to Doc from time to time. Darling took a red Solo cup from his table, scooped in a handful of ice and made Doc a Crown and Coke. Doc sat his bottle of Jack, in its paper bag, beside his chair leg, nodded his thanks and took his first drink of the evening.

It took a few more minutes before Sal came waddling over with his bucket and four Cokes. He sat them all on the table and introductions were exchanged again. There was a sour look—shock or disgust—on the face of Mrs. McDole, as she nodded at Sal. Mrs. Darling couldn't have been more disarming as she offered her hand across the table and Sal gave it a light shake.

Never at a loss, Sal said, "Damn! Darlene Darling. That's one hell of a name," and that got a laugh from the Darlings and Representative McDole.

The four men were at one end of the table and band hadn't started yet. Doc had some questions. "Mr. Darling I was . . ."

"Hold up right there. Just call me Jack. Everybody does."

"Jack, how did you know about us? I mean, none of the stuff that happened has been in the newspapers or on TV or anything."

"That's where you're wrong. The Austin Statesman this morning had a blurb about the girl jumping. But that isn't where I heard about you first. Had lunch with Sheriff Hillman today. I guess y'all had a meeting at his office. Anyway, he told me about the two of you and about your van getting shot up last night. Hell of a thing! We don't get much of that kind of excitement around these parts. I'd wager that half of the people in this place have heard the story—or somebody's fanciful version of it."

Sal said, "Maybe that's why everybody has been gawking at us since we drove up outside."

"Well, the two of you are strangers, on top of it all, and that van . . . well, we don't see many like that these days. At least, not since the hippie craze settled down. You know, news travels fast in a place like LaGrange."

"Fair enough," said Doc. "I have another question, if you don't mind."

"Shoot. I'll tell you anything I can but that may not be much. I kind of mind my own business most of the time."

"We drove around a bit earlier today. Wanted to take a look at two vehicles that got burned last night. It appears that they were the same two driven by them guys who tried to kill us. There's no way to be sure, I guess. Anyway, we kind of got lost trying to find our way back to LaGrange and out someplace northwest of here, best I can figure, we passed a big metal building and saw your Corvette parked there. I was just wondering if that's one of your places of business."

"Well, I'm pleased that you mentioned it! That place

is going to be one of the finest sporting clays clubs between Houston and San Antonio. Dove season will be starting soon and I'll be hosting some potential members for skeet and trap shooting on the first weekend of dove season. Got a couple of stock tanks on the back of the place and it just gets covered up with white wings and mourning doves," said Darling. He was beaming with pride and tipped his Crown and Coke in Doc's direction.

"That sounds great! I'm not much of a shotgunner, myself, but ol' Sal here is an excellent shooter," replied Doc. Sal just nodded in Darling's direction.

"Look, if you boys are stuck here anyway, why don't y'all come around tomorrow afternoon and bust some clay pigeons with us? Steve will be there and Sheriff Hillman plans on coming out. Probably a couple of other locals will be there. Maybe y'all can solve the mystery about that young woman and I'll show you around."

"I guess we are trapped in Fayette County. If Hillman hasn't released us by then, it sounds like fun." Doc looked at Sal, who was swirling his Jack and Coke with one thick finger. "How 'bout that, Sal?"

"Might be fun. I do love to hear the sound of gunfire, so long as it ain't aimed in my direction," said Sal, and everyone except Mrs. McDole chuckled.

"I'd like for you to see Darlene shoot. You know, she won several sporting clays championships back a few years. Ain't that right, baby?"

Darlene nodded and feigned embarrassment just enough to let everyone know she wasn't embarrassed at all. "I do alright, I guess," was all she said.

The small talk continued. Sheriff Hillman walked by and acknowledged everyone. Darling said, "Pull up a chair, David! We were just talking about shooting some clays tomorrow. That is, if you don't let these men go on their way before then." That was the first time Doc and Sal had heard the Sheriff's first name.

He nodded at them and said, "No, I think we need them to hang around until Monday morning. The state boys would like to have another run at them. Maybe try again to identify the car they saw on Monument Hill." Then he turned to Darling and continued, "I have my wife and some other folks over at my table, so I better get back to them. Just wanted to say howdy. I'll see you out at your place tomorrow at one." And, with that he turned and walked across the very crowded building.

Asleep at the Wheel started the party at a little after eight and the dance floor filled quickly. Their first song was "San Antonio Rose" and the crowd cheered their approval. They kept up a steady stream of old Bob Wills tunes, mixed with other Western Swing and music Doc identified as coming from the 1940s and 1950s. Sal scanned the room for unattached females and started his search for companionship. The women seemed reluctant at first—Sal was used to that—but after he found a willing victim and everyone had the chance to see his skill on the dancefloor he had no problem finding partners. He did the Texas Two-Step, the Cotton Eyed Joe, boogie-woogie, and whatever the song called for. He had no trouble finding a dance partner. By the middle of the second set, Sal had been claimed by a large but attractive, blond, forty-something. Just his type—cherubesque. The big man only returned to Darling's table to refill his whiskey tumbler when it ran dry.

Doc, left his friend to his own pleasure and stayed at the table, nursing his whisky and trying to pick up on conversation between Darling, McDole and the other men who walked by to talk. Several took an immediate interest and Doc had to recount the events several times over the course of the evening. He was even surrounded by a group of friendly but inquisitive locals when he went outside to have a smoke. He didn't really mind but it was getting a little tiresome. Evidently, citizens of Fayette County were starved for entertainment.

When the band went on its break before the final set, Sal came over with the lady he'd met and introduced her to Darling's table. She was a large and happy woman—pretty and outgoing. Darlene Darling had met the woman before as they were both involved in the establishment of a boys and girls club in Fayette County. While they chatted, Sal motioned to Doc and they walked away, out of earshot.

"Hey Doc, I think I'll let you take the van back to the motel, if that's OK with you. Vivian—that's the lady's name—asked me to ride with her back to her place for coffee and something sweet."

"Yeah, I think I know what that means. How are you getting back to the old Riverview?"

"I think she'll give me a ride in the morning, or whenever. She has a friend who has been eyeballing you, but I don't think you'd be interested. Not your type. I told her you had a girlfriend back in San Antone."

"Yeah, not really in the mood for any hanky-panky tonight. Where does Vivian live?"

"She's got a place on a farm between here and LaGrange. Says its closer to there than here. I'll be OK."

"Alright man. Go have yourself a large time."

"Hey! No 'large' cracks about ol' Viv." And they both laughed as Sal tossed Doc the van keys. Sal wished everyone at Darling's table a good evening and accompanied Vivian back to the table she shared with a couple and her friend who wouldn't have interested Doc. Shortly after Asleep at the Wheel started their last set, Doc didn't see his friend on the dance floor. When he looked across the room to Vivian's table, he saw that Sal and his new friend had gone on their way.

Mrs. Darling did ask Doc to dance to a slow number. "Texas Me and You" was one of a very few slow songs the band played. He managed not to trample on her feet and was relieved when it was over, although being held by such a woman made him a bit light-headed. Maybe it was just the whiskey.

Doc stayed until the final song—a rollicking version of "Route 66"—and the SPJST hall started clearing out fast. Doc walked back to the Darlings' Corvette with the couple. He was in no rush to try to drive away. The roadway was clogged, bumper to bumper with inebriated locals and Doc was willing to let things thin out before trying to find his way back to LaGrange. "I guess Sal and I will see you tomorrow, if the invitation is still on."

"Absolutely! We have plenty of shotguns, lots of shells and cases of clays. We will start things up around one. See you then," said Jack Darling as he ducked into the driver's seat and closed his door. Mrs. Darling stood by her door a moment longer and smiled at Doc. She looked too deeply into his eyes.

His getaway was slow because of the traffic, and he didn't arrive back at the Riverview until a little after midnight. He noted that a deputy's cruiser was parked on the curb across from the motel entry. It had been a long day and his sleep came easy and without dreams.

***

7.

Doc was sleeping soundly until he was rudely awakened by pounding on the door of room 29. He sat up with a start and felt a pressing pain above his eyes than ran all the way back to his neck. Too much whiskey! The pounding continued and it hurt. "Hold on, dammit! I'm coming." He knew before opening the door that it was Fat Sally. He unlocked the door and was pushed back as the big man forced his way through the doorway.

"Lock the damn door!"

"What the fuck? Is somebody after you?"

"That woman tried to kill me. Let me lay down," said Sal as he crashed onto his bed.

"What in the hell? What did she do? Are you OK?"

"I'll live, I think." Sal was breathing hard. "Old Viv just looked like a soft lady, but she was strong. Reminded me of Croce's Roller Derby Queen. You could roller skate on the bitch. She was insatiable. Wore me out, plumb. I ain't slept a minute." He was laughing now.

Doc's head was still pounding but he managed a chuckle. "Man, I have known you to be with lots of women—I mean, a lot—and I never saw one beat you down."

"Well, you have now. I need a little sleep before we go shoot any guns. I'll tell you all about it sometime."

"OK, you sleep while I get cleaned up. I'll try to find us some breakfast in a little while."

Doc found his dopp kit and dug out a variety of vitamins and three Excedrin and washed them all down with a handful of tap water. He found some clean clothes and laid them out on his bed and jumped in the shower, letting the hot water run over his throbbing head for a long time. When he came out of the bathroom, Sal was snoring loud enough to rattle the windows. Doc knew his friend would be out for a while. He dressed and walked out, locking the door behind him.

He drove to the shop operated by the two elderly Czech ladies on the town square, but they were closed on a Sunday morning, as he expected. When he drove back past the Riverview, he noticed that the deputy car was no longer on protection—or surveillance—detail. He went to the truck stop cafe, which was open, and picked up a beautiful pastry, slathered in vanilla icing, and two large Styrofoam cups of coffee. He popped plastic lids on and squeezed the cups into a cardboard carrier, so as not to foul the shag carpet in the van on the trip back to the motel. Sal was still sleeping when Doc snuck back through the door. He need not worry—his friend was out cold and still snoring at a high decibel level. He sat the food on the little round table and turned on the TV, hoping for some morning news. No cable at the motel and the programming on the three stations involved preachers, trying their best to save his soul with slightly differing approaches. He gave up and just turned it off. It was not yet 7:00am.

Doc and Sal had been friends for twenty-four years—since 1972—and they had enjoyed adventures and suffered through hard times with their friendship never wavering. Even so, their lives had taken different paths.

Doc had an earned an advanced degree before losing interest in academia. His becoming a biker was an unlikely lifestyle change that no one but he understood. He emerged from the biker lifestyle to become a leader in his field. He had worked diligently, always for the same company, to become financially comfortable, if not truly wealthy. If he stayed the course, that might come with time. He lived a solitary life, for the most part, having many acquaintances but few true friends. Even though he was an open book with almost everyone, he could only share his most private thoughts with Sal. That is the mark of true friendship.

For Sal, the big surprise was that he had managed to live to middle age. He came from money. His father built a very successful wholesale grocery empire in the town of Sanctuary. His mother was the from one of the most prosperous families in Scotland. His parents had met and married during WWII. Sal was a problem child, shuffled from school to school because of bad attitude—not for want of intelligence. He had gone to war, been wounded, and he had seen the worst side of humanity. The deepest scars were in his mind and not on his body. After Vietnam, he had lived an aimless life. He squandered a small fortune left to him by his wealthy Scottish grandmother. After several half-hearted attempts at college, he studied drafting, and he was good at it. He married his biker girlfriend, Lois. They had a son, who was now grown and struggling to find his own way. Though he had not lived the biker lifestyle for many years, he never lost the attitude. He still kept a bike and rode when he could. No more customized Harley Davidsons—just a dependable Honda 750.

As dedicated to career as Doc had become, Sal viewed any job as a necessary evil, its only value being to keep the wolf away from his door. Doc was strongly built, down in weight from his college linebacker size, but still 200 pounds on his six-foot frame. Sal had also been an athlete but loved the excesses life offered. He was two inches taller than Doc and now well over 325. Doc dressed for success, whether in a suit or starched Wranglers. Sal could care less what anyone thought of his appearance—what you see is what you get—although he would make some accommodation for the ladies. Both men were fifty now and neither looked to their future with any great anticipation. They would try to live in the moment and wring as much enjoyment out of life as possible. They recognized the other's shortcomings but didn't let them get in the way of their friendship. Neither had a sibling but they both felt the other man was his brother.

***

Doc was in deep thought about their current circumstances—the girl, the car, the shooting. Sitting at the little table and munching chunks of the freshly baked, sweet pastry and drinking his coffee he became drowsy. Coffee never kept Doc awake. He sat his half-empty cup on the table and, still sitting upright, nodded off for another hour, as Sal continued to snore. When he awoke, he was surprised that he had slept so long.

"Hey, Sal! You gonna sleep all damn day?"

The big man grumbled, rolled over, and opened one eye. "Did you scare up some breakfast?"

"Yeah, it was damn good, too. You should have been here to enjoy it." Sal opened the other eye and looked around the room. Doc continued, "Just kidding. I left most of this coffee cake, or whatever it is, for you. Tastes great. But your coffee may be cold by now."

Sal eventually managed to get up, eat the pastry, drink his cold coffee and wander into the bathroom for his morning ritual. They were both presentable and ready to create some gun smoke by 11:30 and they walked out to greet the day.

They stopped by the truck stop café. Sal wanted real food and he picked up two bacon and egg biscuits and washed them down with a beer as they went to hunt for the shooting club. Doc drove and Sal napped after his second breakfast. The drive required that they retrace the route from the previous day, which was not the most direct method. Doc had to backtrack twice but finally saw the tree line and big metal building in the distance. Even with Doc's driving misadventures, they arrived before the designated meeting time. That was OK because Darling's Vette and several other vehicles were already there—all but one being upscale pickups and SUVs.

Doc woke Sal and they walked to the building. The big sliding doors were open on both ends of the building and the midday breeze wafted through. They could see Darling, Sheriff Hillman, and State Representative McDole standing in the middle of the building's expanse. Darling looked over and smiled when he heard them and walked toward Doc and Sal with his hand extended. "I'm happy to see you boys were able to make it. Let me show you around the place."

There were guest rooms on the ground level and along a walkway, a flight of stairs above. Four guestroom doors on each floor and each had a double window looking out onto the building's interior. They looked like standard, mid-range motel rooms.

Darlene Darling was exiting the end room on the lower level. She aimed a broad, welcoming smile at Doc. She walked over and gave both Sal and Doc quick hugs but lingered a bit longer with her arms around Doc's neck. "You fellows ready to do some serious clay bustin'?" She was dressed in stone-washed, starched Wranglers that looked to have been painted onto her legs and backside. The jeans were tucked inside low-heeled, short boots that appeared to Doc to be custom made. She wore a white, short-sleeve huntress shirt with puff sleeves and shooter's pads on the shoulders. Her long, blond hair was pulled into a ponytail with a pair of shooters' glasses perched on top. Her makeup was perfect. She looked expensive, even without any jewelry, and younger than she had the night before. Doc had known women like her before—heading for forty, rich, well-kept, beautiful, and full of confidence.

There was no way not to like what he saw.

The Darlings walked them through one of the guest rooms and they were impressed. It was small but rustic and well-appointed with hunting pictures on the walls. Each room had a private bath. There was an air conditioner mounted below the window. It was as if Darling had built an eight-room hotel inside his big metal building.

"This is a great facility, Jack. What was the building before you had all this work done?" Doc asked.

"It was equipment storage for a construction company. The shell was solid and made to last a hundred years. Just had to build the rooms on one side, lay some clean concrete on the floor and put in kitchen stuff over there," he said, pointing at stainless steel, full setup with large freezer, two refrigerators, oven and cook-top with burners and deep fryer and a big, double sink. It looked unused, like a sparkling new restaurant kitchen. At one end was a small, galvanized livestock trough filled with ice, beer and soft drinks.

"Impressive! I've been to some hunting camps and the like and this tops any of them," said Doc.

Sal nodded and said, "Holy shit! This is some fine shootin' club."

"We are waiting on a couple more guests and then we can get down to some serious shotgunning. Let me show you the range." said Darling. He led them out the big back doorway. There were two shooting towers—steps up to a six-foot high platform with wooden railings. There was a row of target throwing machines, each one packed with stacks of bright orange clays. There were also concrete pads for ground-level shooting. A large Mexican man was arranging shotguns in racks located behind the shooting towers. There were over/under models, semi-automatics, double-barreled, and pump guns in a variety of gauges. Darling was beaming with pride as he showed off his possessions. Sal looked at Doc with a slight shake of his head. Doc knew that was the big man's "Hang the rich" look.

After inspecting everything, they walked back into the building where three more men had arrived and were speaking with the Sheriff and State Rep. Darling introduced everyone and offered them a drink or beer. Everyone asked for a beer, except Darlene and Steve McDole, who opted for Dr Peppers. He said white wings—bacon wrapped, cheese and jalapeno stuffed chicken breast—and other snacks would be served after the shooting. A graying Mexican woman had appeared and was working in the kitchen area.

"OK, let's go bust some clay. Everybody got eyes and ears?" asked Darling, referring to shooting glasses and ear muffs. Only the Darlings and Sheriff Hillman had them, so Darlene went into one of the rooms and brought back a box. Everyone picked out what they needed. Darlene had put on a shooting vest—white with "Austin Women's Clays Champion 1994" embroidered above her left breast. Several of the men, including Darling, also donned vests with pockets and shell holders but none of them advertised championships.

"This is Sam Valdez. He will be running the show," said Darling, introducing the large Mexican man. He proved to be an expert at operating the machines throwing the clay disks. The shooting started and went on for two hours. First, they shot from the ground level pads. Everyone made 20 shots. The first six were at single clays and the remaining in two-target groups. They took turns shooting. Everyone except Sal and Darlene Darling fired 12-gauge guns. Sal chose a Browning 20 gauge over and under and Mrs. Darling was using her custom 28-gauge, side-by-side gun. Doc and one other man were the amateurs of the group, managing only six hits in their 20 chances. Sal hit 18 out of 20—all six singles but he missed two of the doubles.

Darlene's skill was amazing. She hit all 20, even though the 28-gauge required a much higher degree of accuracy. It was easy to see why she was a champion. Of the rest of the group, Hillman and another man scored well with the others, including Jack Darling, having less success.

They broke for smokes and fresh drinks before shooting from the towers. The results were much the same as from the ground, although Doc did manage nine hits out of his 20. Sal missed only one and Darlene again busted every target. She was unhappy because one of her clay pigeons took only one pellet, knocking off a chip and flipping the clay, but it still counted as a hit.

After the shooting was done, everyone retreated from the afternoon sun, into the shade of the building. Two big floor fans had been turned on to help mitigate the summer heat and it was comfortable. As they walked back in, Mrs. McDole was arriving in a chauffeured black sedan, and she walked to her husband and put her arm around his waist.

A serving table had been set up with a large tray of the grilled white wings, a platter of cheeses and baskets with a variety of crackers and bowls of mixed nuts. A full bar had also appeared and several people mixed themselves drinks. Everyone was left to their own devices, and they clustered into twos and threes, seated at one of the two folding tables or standing and talking about whatever.

Doc and Sal stood in front of one of the big fans, enjoying the cool. "This is quite a place, ain't it. He's got to have a reason for this. I mean, you don't just build something like this so your friends can have a place to bust clays and shoot doves," was Sal's take on the place.

"I think he plans to start a club and it won't be cheap to join. Heard them talking last night. While you were courting the roller derby queen."

Sal elbowed his friend and said, "Go to hell! What

else did you hear?"

"Darling and McDole were saying something about bringing down groups from the legislature for outings. I believe he also wants to make it available for companies to lease for junkets. He said he would start promoting it all this winter and he hopes to have lots of bookings by spring."

"I'm going to get me some more of them little chicken things and find a place to sit down. I'm getting sore. Last night was a workout."

Doc had an uncanny skill for remembering lyrics. He laughed as Sal walked away and sang,

"She is a five foot six and two fifteen
A bleached-blonde mama with a streak of mean
She knew how to knuckle
And she knew how to scuffle and fight
And the roller derby program said
That she were built like a 'fridgerator with a head
The fans called her Tuffy
But all her buddies called her Spike"

Sal looked back over his shoulder, shot Doc the bird and mouthed, "Fuck you." He walked back to the serving table and struck up a conversation with one of the men grazing there.

Darlene appeared beside Doc, bumped him with her hip, and said, "How are you enjoying the day?"

"This is quite an operation. Of course, I can't shoot worth a damn. I'm better with a rifle. I'm impressed. I guess y'all have some groups coming in for shooting and dove hunting this season."

"That's Jack's thing. Yeah, he has at least a few groups scheduled. I don't think he has it thought out very well yet. I will skip most of them. Don't like to be the only woman for a bunch of old reprobates to ogle. He might arrange for some companionship for important people, if you know what I mean. I know I don't want to be here when that happens. I like to get out on my own some and that kind of thing gives me the chance."

Doc was shocked that the woman would be so open with a stranger. He didn't know how to respond so he just nodded and said, "Well, I wish him well with his plans."

"You live in San Antonio, right?"

"Yes ma'am. Been there off and on for over twenty years. I may have to relocate to my corporate office in Chicago again sometime in the next year."

"You can drop that ma'am shit right now! We have danced together and hugged and that means you know me well enough to call me Darlene. Got that?"

"Yes ma . . . yes, Darlene." And they both laughed.

"We have a time share in San Antonio. On the River Walk. Maybe we could have dinner or a drink or something when I'm in town. I think I'd like that," she nudged him with her elbow, and he was surprised again.

"I'm sure it would be great but wouldn't Jack find a problem in that? I mean, I'm a single man and you are a beautiful lady. I wouldn't want to cause you or Jack any problems."

Her laugh was like music and put her hand on his shoulder. "Doc, I didn't ask you to take me to bed. Just an innocent dinner, maybe."

"Sorry. I didn't mean to be forward," Doc stammered.

"Oh, stop it! You need to know that I am my own woman. Jack does his thing and I do my thing and, sometimes, we do a thing together. He likes to play little games and sometimes I don't mind joining in. I would like to get to know you better. Maybe something would come of it and maybe it wouldn't. Might be interesting," she said, bumped him with her hip again and strolled away. It wasn't possible for him to take his eyes off her retreat. He glanced toward Jack and saw that his back was turned he was in deep conversation with McDole and two other men.

Doc and Sal made their thank-yous and left while the sun was on the western horizon. But not before Darlene gave Doc another hug with a pinch of his earlobe.

Back in the van, Sal said, "What the hell's goin' on with you and the pretty lady? You gettin' frisky on me Doc?"

"Man, you got me! What a woman. Good looking and she can shoot. Suppose she has a boat?"

"If she has a boat, that would be the clincher. We'd just have to get rid of ol' Jack."

Later, Doc said, "You were gonna tell me about your night. Tell me all about Viv and how she did this much damage to you. You are getting old, brother."

"I don't want to talk about it. Yeah, I guess I'm getting old. She wanted to pick me up after she goes to dinner tonight with her ex-in-laws. Do you believe that?"

"About wanting to pick you up or about her ex-in-laws. Both options are equally confusing," said Doc and he couldn't keep from laughing at his friend.

"I'm confused too. If she comes knocking, just play possum. OK?"

"Yeah. We don't need no extracurricular activities tonight. We gotta be at Hillman's office at 8:00am. Maybe he will turn us loose and we can go walk through some wineries."

***

8.

Doc and Sal made an early night of it. They ate their dinner at the Mexican restaurant again and turned in early. Viv did not knock on their door and Sal was relieved. They flipped between '60 Minutes' and 'Dateline' and found nothing of interest to watch so they just turned off the TV.

Doc had left a wake-up call request with the motel office, and it came at 6:00am. "Let's get some real breakfast this morning. I bet the truck stop place has a good one. The biscuits I had yesterday were good," said Sal so they cleaned up and drove the short distance to the café. A rotund lady with a vague German accent took their orders and they feasted on cat-head biscuits, cream gravy loaded with sausage and over-easy eggs. Both were stuffed by 7:45 when they headed out for the meeting at Sheriff Hillman's office.

A female deputy directed them back to the same room where they had met on Saturday morning. The room was empty, and she said, "Everybody should be here in a bit. There's coffee and kolaches in the kitchen."

"Thank you, ma'am, but we just ate. Might grab a cup of coffee though," said Sal. When she was out of earshot, he looked at Doc and said, "Best looking deputy sheriff I ever saw. Beats the hell out of that miserable Schaer." And they laughed.

After a few minutes wait, Hillman, Naiser and a pleasant looking, nicely dressed black lady entered the room. Naiser spoke, "Guys, this lady is Dr. Margaret Spears. She's a psychologist. She works with our office, from time to time, when we are trying to solve crimes. We'd like for you two to talk to her. Maybe she can help you recall some things before you get out of town." Spears walked around the table, took a tape recorder from her large purse, and sat it down without pressing the 'record' button. Naiser and Hillman walked back out and shut the door.

"A psychologist? We may be half a bubble off of plumb, but I don't think we need a psychologist," said Sal, with a big smile and in good spirits.

She laughed and said, "I heard you two were a couple of cards! I don't think you are crazy—not yet at least. The reason Major Naiser and his supervisor asked me to talk to you is that maybe I can help you remember more about the incident up at the park. Sometimes details are hidden, sort of in the back of your mind and talking about them in a stress-free way can help you to remember. That's all. Are you both alright with talking to me?"

"Dr. Spears, this isn't going to involve hypnotism, is it? I have had that tried on me a couple of times and it just didn't take," said Doc.

"That would be an option but, no, I don't think we need to go down that path."

"Hell, I can be hypnotized in a heartbeat. Pretty good party trick. I don't mind you giving it a try on me if you want to," said Sal and Doc laughed but Spears didn't.

"Let's just see how it goes. I'll want to speak to each of you individually. We can close the shades to make the room as dark and comfortable as possible and just have a talk. Who wants to go first?"

"Sal can go first. You be good now, Sal. Don't give the good doctor any trouble and don't make no passes," said Doc and Sal showed him his middle finger. Doc walked out, leaving Sal with the doctor. He went down the hall, poured himself a cup of coffee, and sat at the kitchen table, across from the attractive deputy. "Tell me all about being a deputy sheriff in LaGrange, Texas," Doc said, and she did.

An hour later, Sal and Dr. Spears walked into the kitchen. "Well, how did that go?" Doc asked.

Spears looked at Sal and said, "Well, I was able to get a good picture of the girl running and going over the cliff and some of the language the man in the car used. I'm going to take a little break and then, Mr. Quinn, we can have a little talk."

Dr. Spears walked out, toward the restroom, Sal said, "She did hypnotize me. Piece o' cake. I can go under like nobody's business. I think I did remember exactly what the guy hollered at the girl, while I was under. Don't know that it helped. Just a lot of cussing and threatening in Spanish. I understand the jibber-jabber pretty good but don't speak it very good."

"Well, I am pretty basic with it—*hablo un poquito y comprendo poco mas*. So you were able to tell her more than I could on that."

"She went and got a big book with pictures of cars and tried to get me to pick out what the guy was driving. I couldn't do no good with that. The guy and the car were just a blur with me, if I even saw them, at all. I think you got a better look."

"Maybe so. I'll take a look at her book but I'm not going for being hypnotized. Tried it before and it don't work on me. How did it feel?"

"Really kind of just don't remember much about it. Hope she didn't take advantage of me while she had me under. I'd hope to remember that." Sal said, smiling.

"You are such a damn kid! Grow the fuck up."

Dr. Spears came back into the kitchen, poured herself a cup of coffee and wiggled her finger at Doc, who followed her back into the meeting room. They sat on opposite sides of the table and Spears said, "I've heard Mr. Lombardo's telling of the incident and it matches well with the recording that was made earlier. I'd like for us to concentrate on the vehicle and the man driving it. Please tell me as much as you recall."

Doc gave her, almost word for word, what he had described earlier. When he finished, she said, "Let's concentrate on the car. Before, you said it might be an older Chevrolet sedan, two-door or hardtop model, I believe. By the 70s and 80s, a lot of cars sort of had similar profiles, regardless of make or model. You know, unless they were compacts or station wagons or something unusual. Let's look at some pictures of cars, and maybe something will sharpen your recollection."

"OK, let's give it a try," said Doc, but he thought the effort might be fruitless. A thick album was on the corner of the table, and she pushed it to a point between them, right side up for Doc, and shuffled through the pages until she reached 1970s models of many automobiles. She turned pages until she found models similar to his earlier description—2-door sportier sedans. He looked at pictures for a half-hour with nothing jumping off the page.

"Like I said, cars all looked a little alike back then. Not as much as now. Hell, now you can't tell the difference between a Mercedes and a Ford," she said, shaking her head. "Let's move forward a bit." And she shuffled more pages.

Doc still didn't find anything that clicked with him but he did keep going back to the photo of a 1980 Pontiac Grand Am. There was something about it that he couldn't quite place but it was familiar, somehow. He looked at cars for most of an hour and finally said, "I'm sorry but I don't think this is doing any good. The profile of a lot of these cars is in the ballpark but I can't point at one in particular and say that's it."

"That's alright. Maybe something will come to you later. Let's talk about the man who was driving. Did you assume he was Hispanic based on what he was saying, or did you get a good enough look to recognize his general type—young or old, tall or short, thick or thin?"

"I can tell you that I don't think he was a large man. Certainly not heavy set. Best I could tell, he was in a white or light colored, long-sleeve shirt, and dark pants. Come to think of it, I don't think he was wearing blue jeans. Maybe black pants, kind of loose fitting? He had dark hair—but then, it was still not full daylight yet. Anything but blond or bald might have looked dark. He was only out of the car for a few seconds, hollering at the girl."

"I noticed from the earlier recording that you didn't indicate which direction the car had come from. I think you said it took off down the road to the left. Did you see where he came from?"

"Well, nobody asked. I think everyone took for granted that he came and went to and from the left. To the right is into that sharp curve and the houses up there. A residential neighborhood. You know, I have the feeling that he came from the right, for some reason. I believe he might have turned a donut in the parking lot because he stirred up a lot of dust and the driver's side was toward us when the girl jumped out the passenger side. She must have run around the back of the car before she headed into the park."

"OK, as you were just picturing it in your head, did you get anything more on the car?"

"Not really."

"Well, if you think of anything, let Sheriff Hillman know. Sometimes things come back to us or we see something that spurs a memory."

"Will do," Doc said but he didn't have confidence that he would dredge up any new images.

Before Doc and Sal left the sheriff's office, Hillman joined them in the reception area. "Well, did you ol' boys come up with anything new? I hear that Dr. Spears is pretty good at what she does."

"She recorded everything. The only thing I really thought of was that I believe the car was coming from the right side—from the direction of the fancy houses—rather than from the highway side. Don't know if that means anything or not," said Doc.

"You think on that one for a while because it seems pretty unlikely to me. I mean, there's no easy route from any main road, through the residential streets. I guess it could happen but not unless the guy knew the area. And I'm pretty sure there's no den of outlaws hanging out in that neighborhood," replied the Sheriff.

"She hypnotized me so I'm not sure what all I might have told her. Don't let none of it get back to my wife," said Sal.

Hillman chuckled and handed both of them his card. "I reckon I shouldn't hold you fellows any longer. I think y'all have done everything you could. If we get any information about the girl or need anything, we can call you. Same for the men who shot up your vehicle. I don't suppose either of you have a cellular telephone? Anyway, leave your addresses and home and work numbers with Deputy Hlavinka before you go." He pointed at the attractive deputy manning the desk.

"I've got a cellular phone that I use for work, but I don't take it on vacation. I'll leave that and my home and office number," said Doc. They left the requested information and walked out.

***

9.

"Do you think we will hear anything from them," Sal asked as he drove toward Hwy 71.

"Probably not. This has been three days we ain't never gonna get back. Of course, you do have a bunch of souvenirs of all the fun we have had, between the holes in the van and any scars ol' Viv laid on you."

Sal didn't bother to reply.

"Let's get back on plan. We wasted most of our run-away time, but I'd like to ride up to Tow on Lake Buchanan. Supposed to be one of the nicest wineries in the state. I had some of their Sauvignon Blanc at a dinner a while back and I swear it was the best white wine I ever drank. The place is called Fall Creek Vineyards."

Sal responded, "The best white wine I ever drank was Boone's Farm Apple. Easy to down, sweet, cheap, and gave a hell of a bad head the morning after."

"Sounds like you are describing most of the women I've ever known you to go for. Well, obviously excepting Lois."

"That too. We need to get us one of them cellular phones. I know some guys who have them. Bad thing is, you can't get away from everyone if you are carrying one of those," said Sal.

"I don't like mine. Only carry it when I'm on the clock. Got that and a damn pager and ignore both of them most of the time. The phone only works when you are in certain areas. I guess they are OK around bigger towns, but they would be worthless out in the boonies. They say everybody will be carrying them in a couple of years. Don't know if that sounds like progress or not."

They rode across the north Colorado bridge and onto the new pavement that would connect with a bypass around LaGrange, which was still under construction. Hwy 71 would take them to Bastrop and, eventually to Austin. They passed the LaGrange airstrip and made the swing around the little settlement of Plum. Doc was looking out the window with nothing particular on his mind. A couple of miles farther on he saw something that got his full attention.

"Sal, Slow down!"

"What the fuck? What did you see?"

"I'm not sure. There is a little truck stop just up the road. Pull in there and turn around. I want to take a look at something."

Sal made a loop in the truck stop's lot and then he nosed back on to the highway. "Drive slow and take a left at that next road." Sal made the turn and, just a hundred yards down there was an old house. It looked like it had been built onto more than once but not for many years. It was sprawling, like many older ranch houses, with a stained tin roof and a separate garage with hinged wooden doors—open. Parked and with only the front bumper behind the left door was a black car with a red strip down the side, below the chrome line. "Keep driving on past. That's the car I saw. It's just like a Pontiac in Dr. Spears' book—red paint and all. I knew the picture looked familiar."

They both stared at the house and car as Sal slowly drove past. As they got just beyond the garage, they could see someone exit the house and walk toward the car but couldn't tell anything about him. "Keep driving, like we have someplace to go."

"Man, are you sure? You really think that's what the

car looked like?" asked Sal.

"It's the first thing I've seen that snapped for me. Just drive on down past that tree line. Looks like the road curves there."

"If we had us one of them portable phones, we could call the law." Sal wasn't taking this whole diversion very seriously. "I think you have an overactive imagination. That's what I think."

There was a field entry path past the tree line and Sal pulled in there. It was well out of sight of the house. He wanted to know, "OK Sherlock Holmes, what do we do now?"

"Elementary, my dear Watson. Maybe not elementary. Let's think on it a bit. Suppose it was our guy. Or, better yet, suppose I'm totally fucked up and it wasn't the car, at all. We don't want to go crying 'wolf' to the cops." They sat quietly for several minutes and then Doc said, "Hell, let's just go back and knock on the door. Asking for directions. We are lost and looking for—who?"

"Half the folks around here have Bohemian names and the other half are German. Pick a name. Well, I guess about half of them have Mexican names, too," said Sal. "I ain't too proud to walk up and knock on the door and ask if this is the Hlavinka place. Might get lucky. Maybe the deputy's mama looks just like her and she's at home."

"You haven't changed a bit. Got nookie on your mind all the time."

"Don't make me all bad. You can't tell me that you didn't get a little interested, looking at that woman in uniform. OK, let's go find out." With that, he backed onto the gravel road and drove toward the house. The car they had seen was gone.

Sal pulled the van into the driveway and stopped in front of the garage—its doors now closed with a 2X4 holding them in place. They got out and Sal mounted the concrete steps to the front porch and knocked on the door while Doc tried to take a look through a window. He couldn't see anything. Nobody came to the door but both men heard a rattle inside the house.

"I think there's somebody in there. Knock again," said Doc and he walked around the left side of the house and tried another window, still with no luck. There were three window air conditioners mounted along the expanse of the wall and they blocked any hope of seeing inside. Sal was still at the front door when Doc walked back around. Just then they saw the black and red car turning off Hwy 71. Behind it was a light blue Crown Vic—the same one Schaer had used to follow them on Saturday. The Pontiac pulled into the driveway, tight to the van's rear bumper, and the Ford drove right into the weeds of the front yard.

"What are you two fellows up to? Thought Sheriff Hillman sent you on your way," said Schaer through his rolled down window. The other man was still inside the Pontiac.

"We were just kind of lost. Looking for a lady's house. Met her at the SPJST dance the other night," said Sal as he edged from the doorstep and started walking toward the van. Doc froze where he stood at the corner of the house.

Shaer lifted his .45 auto and pointed it out his car window. "Fat man, you stay right where you are. You move and I'll shoot you." Sal stopped and glared at the deputy. Doc took two steps toward the van and held his ground when he saw the pistol.

"Santos, look in that piece of shit van and see if you can find a gun. I know they got at least one." The man exited the Pontiac, walked to the passenger door of Sal's van, checked the glove box, and immediately found Sal's 1911.

"Got it!" said Santos and he stuffed it in his belt

behind his back. As an afterthought, he walked back to his car, reached under the driver's seat, and collected his own revolver—an old snub-nose Smith and Wesson .38.

Schaer still held his gun on Sal. He said, "What the hell are we gonna do with y'all now?" He carefully exited his car and reached back through the window, taking out two pairs of handcuffs. He pitched the cuffs toward Santos, and they landed in the dust. "Let's get these two out of sight. You think you can manage to shackle these guys without fucking it up?"

"I think I can handle that," said the man, with a heavy Spanish accent, as he picked up the manacles and walked toward Sal.

"One pair of handcuffs ain't gonna get it done," said Sal. "You'll need both sets for me. One ain't long enough. I know. It might surprise you that this ain't the first fucking time somebody but chains on me. Or the first time some asshole held a gun on me. And, if this little bastard gets too close to me, I'll just snap him like twig. You hearing me?" he said to Schaer.

The deputy shifted his aim to Doc and said, "Lardass, you best be nice. You fuck up and I'll put your buddy down like a dog. *You* hearing me?"

The standoff only lasted a few seconds but seemed longer to them all. Then Schaer said, "Go ahead and lock up the fat man. I have more cuffs in the car." Schaer stood, maintaining a two-handed aim at Doc's chest while Santos locked one of the cuffs around each of Sal's wrists—he could only make them engage a single click because Sal's wrists were so large—then he attached the other rings of the cuffs together behind Sal's back. Santos backed away and aimed his own gun at Sal while Schaer opened the Crown Vic's trunk and took out a shotgun and another set of handcuffs. He tossed the cuffs to Santos, who chained Doc's hands behind his back.

"Let's get out of this broad daylight! Nobody needs to see what's going on here," said Schaer. With Santos in the lead and unlocking the front door, they walked into the cool of a shabby living room. "Sit you asses down on that davenport while I figure out what to do with you." Both men flopped uncomfortably down on the faded, sagging sofa.

Sal said, "Well you got us in the shit again, didn't you Doc?"

"Looks like. Never was no shit quite like this, though," was Doc's answer.

Schaer sent Santos back out to pull the van into the garage, while he considered his next move. He was a toady who couldn't make any decisions and, as much as he wanted to be a big shot, he knew that wasn't his fate. He would have to get his instructions from higher up.

***

When Santos got back from hiding the van, he walked down a hall to the rear of the rambling house. Doc and Sal heard him speaking to someone in Spanish. That had to be the same someone they overheard when Sal knocked on the door.

Schaer was slouching in an overstuffed chair across the room from them, still holding his gun in them. He knew it would take time and effort for them to extricate themselves from the soft, low couch and become a threat to him, so he had calmed considerably but he looked from one to the other with his tiny blue eyes. His wheels were turning.

"Well Deputy Schaer, shouldn't you be out protecting the citizens of Fayette County? Somebody's probably gonna miss you if you hang around here too long," Doc finally said.

"You don't need to worry about that. I work Saturdays and have Sunday and Monday off. I'm on my own today."

Sal asked, "Were you on duty while you were following us all over the county on Saturday?"

"What do you mean?" asked Schaer.

"Bullshit! Did you think we didn't see you following us around. Nobody's that dumb. With that spotlight on the door, it was easy to tell it was a cop car." said Sal.

"Well, as a matter of fact, I was. David wanted me to keep an eye on you two. He didn't want anybody shooting at you again. Had to protect his two witnesses. By the by, that's no cop car. Not anymore, anyway. It's mine. I bought it at an auction in Columbus. It used to be the Chief's car down there."

"So, I guess our Sheriff is the top dog behind whatever this shit is all about. You waiting to get guidance from him?" asked Doc.

"Hold on there! My brother-in-law is as honest as they come. He's a downright square when it comes to the law. He has nothing to do with anything. I just want you to be straight on that."

Doc thought for a moment and said, "We don't know what any of this is about. We were just in the wrong place at the wrong time. If you hadn't come back here and grabbed us up, we would have been on our way and out of your hair. Why don't you tell us what's going on here? Or, we can still go away and never be seen again."

"I don't believe you boys are long for the world. But I don't make that call. Now that we have you, I can't let you go anywhere. Yeah, I wish Santos hadn't seen your van and called me. It was all a done deal, once that happened. I told him to ditch the Pontiac but it's his only wheels."

"OK then, what is going on here? If you are going to

do us, you might as well tell us," said Sal.

"Fat man, I don't mind telling you some things. You know, I'm fucked if you'd ever get out of this mess you're in."

"Where's the guys who tried to kill us? I'd like a shot at them before I go. I'm pretty pissed about what they did to my classic ride."

Schaer laughed. "Yeah, that one's a classic, alright! Those two were back in Piedras Negras in time to give the priest their Saturday confession. You won't see them again. But, hey, come to think of it, you might wind up across the border yourselves."

Doc said, "We heard noises in the house before you two drove up. What's going on here?"

"Too bad about that. If you hadn't heard nothing, you might have gone on your way before we got back. It's nothing, really. Just some ladies we have doing a little work back in the kitchen. You might say, they're cooking up something special." Schaer said with a chuckle.

"Were you always a piece of shit or did money turn you into one?" asked Sal.

"Think what you want to. I don't give a damn." Then he took a deep breath and said, "You know, I was supposed to be a school teacher. Went to U of H and got a degree to teach history and math. Then my sister married David and he got elected sheriff and he offered me this job. Both teaching and being a deputy pay for shit. It only took me two years of trying to hammer some knowledge into a bunch of eighth graders to let me know it wasn't my calling."

"Seems to me, it would have been safer than being in law enforcement," said Doc.

"When's the last time you spent eight hours a day with a bunch of twelve- and thirteen-year olds? Since they don't want teachers paddling some respect into the little bastards, it's chaos in the classroom."

They sat for a few more minutes and Sal said, "You gotta let me up and take these handcuffs off. I gotta take a shit."

Schaer thought for a minute before answering. Then he said, "I don't want to be in the room with you if you do it in your pants. Gimme a minute." He walked to the hall door, still holding his gun on Doc and Sal. He called out, "Santos, what the hell are you doing? Come here!"

Santos showed up a minute later, still tucking his shirttail into his black dress pants. He was dark with oiled, black hair, and a thin moustache on his perpetually angry face. He was about 5'8" and lean but fit, like a man who had worked hard all his life. He looked to be in his early thirties. "*Chinga*, man! What the fuck you need? I was takin' care of some business," he said, in his thick accent.

Sal looked at Doc and said, "Yep, that's the voice."

"Leave them girls alone! You gonna ruin them. They got work to do," barked Schaer. "The fat man needs to take a shit. You need to take him to the can while I watch the other one."

"Come on, *Gordo*! Get you lard ass up and come with me."

Sal stood, with some effort. With hands behind his back, it was difficult to lift himself from the sagging couch. "You gonna have to take the fucking cuffs off so I can go. Unless you want to undress me, hold my dick and wipe my ass."

"I ain't doin' that! Bobby, what you want me to do?"

"Just get him to the shitter and cuff him to a pipe or faucet or something until he gets done. Shoot the son-of-a-bitch if he gets stupid," said Schaer. Then he looked at Doc and said, "If he gives you any trouble, I'll go ahead and kill this one. You hear that big man?"

"I fuckin' heard you. Now get me to the restroom

before I make a mess."

Schaer thought hard for a moment and then tossed the handcuff key to Santos and said, "OK, unlock one of the empty cuffs and let's hook them in front of him." He kept his aim on Doc as Santos tried to figure out how to do as he was told. He got it done and Sal had the two pair of cuffs with the middles locked in front.

"This way, *cabrõn*." And the Mexican held his .38 tight against Sal's spine and guided him down the hallway. There were three doors on the left side and a solid wall on the right. The hall opened into a large kitchen. There were three women sitting at the table and they hardly looked up, fear painted on their features and avoiding eye contact. One was old—probably only 50 but she had lived a hard life—and two younger women, both attractive but poorly maintained. They sat ridged, moving only their eyes as Santos guided Sal across the room and into a short hall. The home's only bathroom was on the right side and Sal could see the back door of the building at the end of the hall. The toilet was filthy and sat next to a sink attached to the wall with water and drain pipes below. Santos again unhooked one empty bracelet and hooked them together again, around the drain pipe below the sink.

"Do your business, *cabrõn*! I leave the door open."

"Oh man! Close the fucking door. What the hell am I gonna do? I can't shit with you looking at me. For Christ's sake!"

Santos partly closed the door, leaving a six-inch gap. Sal was trying to figure out his next move. With his hands shackled to the pipe, he had to squat close to the sink to unbutton his jeans. He was glad he hadn't worn overalls—undressing, in his current state, would have been impossible. He had to sit sideways on the toilet and his first thought was how he would reach the paper roll which was mounted on the wall to his right side. That was not really an issue because a bowel movement was the last thing on his mind—only part of his subterfuge. The only problem was that he hadn't planned beyond where he currently sat.

Sal Lombardo considered himself the world heavyweight champion of the head butt. In his wilder days, it wasn't unusual for him to knock bikers and cowboys unconscious with the tactic. When he drank brown liquor, he had often instigated contests. His forehead was broad and thick below his tightly curled hair. He knew that if he could get Santos close enough it would be a done deal. His hands being shackled presented the problem. He knew he had to be quiet in whatever he did, even though Schaer was several rooms away, holding his pistol on Doc. He pulled the cuffs tight against the drain pipe and slowly tugged until the U-joint in the pipe disengaged and the water in the trap spilled onto the bathroom floor.

"What are you doin' in there fat man? I don't hear nothin'. Don't be no *pendejo.*"

"It takes me a minute. Just hold your horses. I'll be done when I'm done," Sal said and managed to force out a loud fart.

"I heard that!" said Santos, and he laughed.

"Fuck you."

With his right elbow he bumped the toilet paper roll loud enough for Santos to hear. Then he did it again. "I'm about done here. Give me another minute." He surveyed the little room, looking to complete his plan. There was a dirty towel hanging from a peg next to the sink but no shower curtain rod or towel rack or anything else to use as a weapon. He would have to hope he could manage without one.

"OK. Come in and unhook me," he said, and Santos used his foot to kick open the door. Again, he considered the safest way to manage the job. He tucked his little revolver into his front pocket and edged toward Sal, who was still sitting on the toilet with his jeans around his feet.

"What's this fucking water on the floor? Did you bust somethin'?"

"I can't help it you got leaky pipes. Unhook me, goddamn it."

Santos took the key from his pocket and leaned in to unhook the cuff and Sal sprang. He couldn't muster full force but he butted Santos on the side of his head, crashing against his ear and temple and the other side of the man's head smacked into the sink. At the same time Sal jerked the cuffs and pulled the pipe apart. Santos didn't go down but he was stunned; he grappled for his pistol, but Sal looped the cuffs around the back of the man's neck and jerked his face down into his bare left knee. Blood flew from Santos' nose and Sal pushed him to the floor and put his knee on the man's neck. Then he grabbed the towel and wrapped it around Santos' face and pulled it tight. Santos wasn't out. He flailed his hands, grappling for his pistol but it was in his pocket, under him, and he couldn't reach it. By then Sal was on top of him with his knees in the man's back and his full weight crushing him and making it impossible to breathe. Sal looked around and saw the lid on the back of the toilet. He jerked it up and smashed the heavy porcelain onto the back of Santos' head and the struggle was over. All but Sal falling flat on his stomach, having forgotten that his jeans were around his ankles.

From the front of the house, Sal could hear Schaer yell, "What's going on there. Is everything alright?"

Sal was pulling up his pants and yelled back, using his best Spanish accent, *"Esta bien. Uno momento!"* It must have satisfied the deputy because Sal didn't hear anything more. He got his jeans fastened and surveyed the bathroom. From the blood on the back of Santos' head, he thought the man was dead. He put his hand on Santos back to see if he could feel breathing and he thought he did. He picked up the toilet cover and smashed it again into the man's head. Now, he knew Santos was *muerto*. He gathered himself, found the key and unlatched his shackles, letting them fall on top of the dead man's body. Then he picked up one set of handcuffs and stuffed them in his belt, putting the key in his pocket.

He pulled his own .45 from the back of Santos' pants. Then he rolled him over and reached into his pocket, which was wet from the piss that escaped his bladder at the moment of his demise. He took the .38 and put it in his own pocket and wiped the piss from his hand on the towel around Santos' head. He stepped over the body and walked into the kitchen.

The women's eyes were wide with terror, but they remained silent. Sal put his finger to his lips, letting them know to stay that way. It was only then that he noticed that the older woman's foot was chained and that the chain was locked to an eye-bolt in the floor. There were no restraints on the younger women, although the most attractive one had visible marks on her wrists and ankles. They both looked like they were in their teens—certainly no older than twenty.

He again motioned for them to be quiet and slowly walked into the long hallway. The floor creaked under his bulk, and he knew there was no way for him to use stealth to his advantage. He eased down and pulled the cuffs from his belt and rattled them, just a bit, for effect.

"Santos, get your ass back in here," Schaer called out. Sal rattled the cuffs again and took two more steps toward the open door into the living room. Then he slid his feet along the linoleum rather than stepping down. That had the result he wanted—silent movement the last ten feet to the doorway. He peeked around the door jam and, as expected, saw the deputy's back to him, still seated and pointing his pistol at Doc. Sal raised his 1911 and aimed at the back of

Schaer's head.

"OK deputy, drop your gun or I'll blow you away," Sal said in a calm voice. Schaer jerked around and his right elbow bumped the back of his chair just enough for his shot to just take a hunk of skin from the side of Sal's neck. Sal's aim was better. His bullet ripped through Schaer's body at his shoulder blade and shattered his spine. He slumped, his face showing total surprise.

Doc managed to stand, his ears ringing from the roar of the two .45 blasts. It took him a beat to overcome the stun of the shots and realize that his friend had been shot. Sal stood, still holding his pistol in his right hand and his left pressed to the side of his neck. Then the big man sank to his knees, never releasing his gun or his wound. He looked up at Doc as he shuffled over, his hands still bound behind his back. He kneeled down and faced his friend, helpless without his hands. Sal shook his head, put his pistol on the floor and said, "Turn around. Let me unlock you." His face was losing color quickly and he almost toppled over on Doc but pulled himself back upright, still on his knees. He fished in his pocket and found the key. Doc shuffled around until his back was to Sal and the big man fumbled for almost a minute until he finally got the key in the lock of one of Doc's cuffs and the shackle sprang open.

"Doc, I think I'm fucked up," said Sal and he sagged forward onto his friend and Doc eased him go the floor.

"Hold on brother! Let me get something for you." He stood and looked around. First thinking to rip the shirt from the deputy but it was soaked in blood. "Hold on!" he said again and sprinted down the hall, not knowing what he would find. In the kitchen, he saw the terrified women, still immobile. "I need some towels or something. Help me!" One of the younger women stood and opened a drawer on the cabinet behind where she had been sitting. She pulled a stack of dish towels out and tossed them to Doc. He turned and ran back down the hall to Sal. The young woman followed ten feet behind. She screamed and ran back to the kitchen when she saw the carnage in the living room.

Doc made a thick pad from one towel and used two others, tied together, to make a bandage to hold the first one in place and pulled it as tight as he dare so as not to cut off the blood to Sal's brain. Sal was woozy and about to pass out but managed to say, "Find a phone and call an ambulance. And the Sheriff." And then he passed out.

Doc was in a panic. He put a couch pillow under Sal's head, checked the bandage, and ran through the house. The first of the three rooms on the hallway held only a cast iron bed and dresser but, in the second, he found a full bedroom set with a phone on the bedside table. He listened for a dial tone and there was one. He dialed 0 and the operator said, "Operator. May I help you?"

"Can you route me to the Fayette County Sheriff's office. Please! This is an emergency."

"One moment please."

Ten seconds later, Doc heard the buzz of a phone ringing. "Good Morning. Fayette County Sheriff's Office." It was Deputy Hlavinka.

"Miss Hlavinka, this is Connor Quinn. I need the Sheriff and an ambulance. Quick. I think there are two dead and one wounded. It's a fucking mess!"

"Mr. Quinn, slow down. Tell me where you are."

"Off of 71 northwest of town. The last gravel road before the truck stop. Only house on the road. Schaer's car is parked in the yard. Please send an ambulance quick. Lombardo is wounded. Maybe real bad. Please hurry."

"Are you OK? Is Bobby alright?"

"I'm OK but there's a lot of blood and people down. Hurry!"

"You stay put and try to collect yourself! Stay on the line. I'm gonna put you on hold," and the line went silent.

A very long two minutes later, she came back on and said, "Just keep this line open. I have somebody coming to you. An ambulance and some help." Again it went silent.

Doc ran back into the living room and Sal's eyes were open, but he looked to be catatonic. In shock. "Hold on brother. Cavalry is on the way. Can I get you something?"

No answer but Sal's eyes looked into Doc's. The blood from Sal's neck seemed to be under control, which made Doc relax a bit. He sat by his friend for a minute and then remembered he was supposed to man the phone. He returned to the bedroom and picked up the receiver but there was silence, so he hurried back to Sal's side. It was more than ten minutes later that he heard sirens in the distance and another two before he heard them pull into the yard. He got up and opened the door to see Hillman and two deputies, guns drawn as two state troopers' cruisers were sliding to a stop on the road in front of the house. Doc put his hands up and the Sheriff brushed past him without speaking and halted dead in his tracks.

"Holy shit! What in the hell is going on here?" said Hillman and he turned toward Doc, holding his gun on center mass.

Doc turned to the Sheriff and said, "Hey man, please let the responders get Sal to the hospital. He's bleeding and hurt bad. Please! I'll tell you everything."

Hillman lowered his gun and surveyed the gore, turning a full circle in the room. "Let me sit down. Never seen nothing like this." He was shaken and surveyed the room for a place to sit. Two other deputies, including Johnny Lopez, were standing in the door. They holstered their weapons and just stood, taking in the scene. The ambulance crew pushed through, lugging a gurney. First, they checked Schaer and, realizing he was gone, moved on to Sal.

"We're gonna need some help here. Can't budge this

big guy. Doc and the two deputies helped load and carry Sal to the ambulance. Hillman had just sunk into the couch and removed his hat and was staring at Schaer's body.

Outside, Doc said, "I'm going to the hospital with Sal." And he started to climb into the ambulance.

"Hold up there, Mr. Quinn! I think you need to hang around here for now. I know the Sheriff will need to talk to you," it was Lopez speaking.

Doc looked back and forth from the deputy to the ambulance as the doors were closing. The siren wailed, it pulled back onto the gravel, and sped away, leaving a dusty cloud in the hot summer air.

***

10.

Sheriff Hillman sat on the filthy couch, looking first at the corpse of his brother-in-law and then at his boots, shaking his head. He repeated, "What am I going to tell Alice?" She was his wife and the sister of the dead man.

Five men stood around, taking in the scene for several minutes before Hillman wearily stood and put his Stetson back on his head. "We need to sort this thing out. We should do it here, I guess. Is there any place where we can sit and talk?"

"There's a kitchen table back there," Doc said, pointing toward the hallway. "You need to see that. I don't know what else is back there. Maybe another man. He is out or, maybe, dead."

This got everyone's attention. They all stepped over Schaer's body and around the bloody floor where Sal had fallen. They followed Doc past the bedroom doors, glancing at the telephone, lying silent where Doc had dropped it. In the kitchen, the three women were still in panic mode, huddled together, the older woman with her arms around the two younger ones. Hillman looked around and said, "Are you all OK?"

The women looked at one another but didn't answer. Lopez spoke, "*Hablas ustedes ingles*?"

The older woman responded, "*Un poco*."

Hillman said, "Lopez, take these women into one of the bedrooms and get their story." Lopez motioned them to follow him, and the old woman pointed to the chain around her ankle. "Get the bolt cutters out of my car and cut this woman loose," the Sheriff ordered and the other deputy,

Vacek, ran back out to retrieve them.

While waiting on the bolt cutters, Doc said, "You need to take a look in the bathroom. May be a dead guy in there."

One of the state troopers carefully walked to the bathroom door and peered in. He just nodded back to the other officers and returned to the kitchen. Vacek had the bolt cutters and was clipping the lock that held the chain on the old woman. Then, Lopez motioned the women to follow him as he led them to the room with the phone and closed the door.

There was a pale brown scum on the Formica tabletop and blocks of dope, wrapped in plastic and taped up lying on the counter along with boxes of powdered milk. There were small balloons and glassine bags and plastic sandwich bags on the table, and a small but very sophisticated scale, with tiny counter weights on its tray.

"I guess it's pretty obvious what we have here," said one of the state guys. He continued, "I think we need to call Mr. Naiser or somebody. We need some experts to see this. Probably CDI."

"OK, you go out and get on the radio. The rest of us are gonna sit here and not touch a damn thing in this room. Quinn, it's time for you to tell us what the fuck happened here today," said Hillman. He was still obviously shaken and wondering what he would tell his wife—and everyone else, for that matter.

Over the following hour, Doc related all the events since he and Sal had left the Sheriff's office that morning. Hillman broke in from time to time, still confused about Schaer's place in all this. While he was telling the story, a second ambulance and a hearse arrived and were turned around by the troopers, who said that they didn't want the bodies removed until the CDI people had reviewed the scene. Austin said a team was on its way. This did not please Hillman, who thought that his department should handle the matter.

When Doc finished his telling of the events, Hillman asked, "Are you sure Bobby was involved with the other man? I mean, he's family. And he's a deputy! How could he get caught up in something like this?"

"Sheriff, we were as surprised as anyone could be. If I hadn't seen Santos' car from the highway, we would be on the other side of Austin by now. God! I wish I had never asked Sal to pull over. He thought I was full of shit and I half thought so, myself. That damn car just jumped out at me. I knew I'd seen one just like it in Dr. Spears' book. Like a light came on when I saw it parked here."

"Are you confident the dead man in the bathroom was the same one you saw at Monument Hill?" the Sheriff asked.

"As sure as I can be. I mean, I didn't get any kind of look at him before, except for general type, I guess. His voice was the lock. It was identical to what we heard before the girl jumped."

Johnny Lopez walked back into the kitchen. "I got as much as I could out of them women. They are scared shitless. I guess anybody would be. That Santos guy and some other men brought them here from Piedras Negras over a month ago. Since then, they had been cutting and bagging smack and, excuse my language, they had been getting fucked by several guys on a regular basis. They said the junk made them sick at first but got past it. Also, one of them was forced to go with Santos to someone's house and do sex acts and what sounds to me like some kind of bondage thing. She was the prettiest of the younger women. She said there was another woman who she called Victoria who went away with Santos a few days ago and didn't come back. Obviously, that was the girl who jumped."

"Why did they keep the old woman chained up but not the other two?" Vacek asked and Hillman looked at him as if to say he was the one who was supposed to ask the questions.

"The girls—all three of them—worked at a brothel down south and the *mamacita* was the one who sort of looked out for them. As long as she couldn't run, they knew the girls wouldn't leave the old woman," said Lopez.

Just then, John Naiser walked into the kitchen and looked around. Everyone just stared at him until he said, "This ain't no place to be doing an interrogation. Sheriff, what the hell were you thinking?" The comment hung in the air for a long moment. Hillman's face turned cold as he clinched his jaw and just stared.

Naiser continued, "The crime scene boys are about fifteen minutes behind me. They are excited as a prom queen. Don't get to handle stuff like this enough to get their juices flowing. Sheriff, let's relocate this tea party down to your office. Don't mess with none of the evidence. Hope you haven't screwed it all up already." And his eyes met Hillman's. Both men were angry.

The group all carefully walked through the house and onto the front porch, avoiding stepping in blood or heroin, and tiptoeing around Bobby Schaer's lifeless body. Johnny Lopez led the women out and they stood, clustered tightly in one corner of the porch. They waited until Deputy Hlavinka came with another vehicle. Everyone else loaded into cars, with Doc in the back seat of Hillman's Suburban. Vacek was in the front seat and turned to talk to Doc. "Nobody said nothing yet, but you and the big guy may be looking at a hearing or something."

Hillman barked, "Why don't you shut the fuck up? You ain't got my job just yet." And the rest of the ride to the Sheriff's Office was quiet. Doc sat, worrying about Sal. Back at the office, one of the troopers, Vacek, and Doc were told to wait in the conference room. The building seemed empty, otherwise. Hillman disappeared into his private office and closed and locked his door. He had to tell his wife that her brother was not only a criminal but dead. That was the hardest call he would ever have to make.

***

Sal was in and out of consciousness on his ride to the hospital. Two EMTs hovered over him and the only time he briefly came fully awake was when one of them inserted the IV into his right arm. "Goddamn! Is that the best you can do?" he bellowed and fell back to the gurney, out again. His next memory was of a dark skinned, very serious doctor aiming the narrow beam of a light into his eyes. He knew he received an injection and then, mercifully, fell into a deep sleep.

It was dark outside when he roused from his sleep. He saw Doc sitting in a chair next to his hospital bed, almost napping, himself. "What the fuck happened?" he croaked, and Doc sprung fully awake.

"You got shot, man! How do you feel?"

"I ain't feeling much of nothing right now. What happened? Did I get that fuckin' weasel?"

"Yeah, but you need to concentrate on getting fixed up."

Sal reached up to his neck and felt the heavy bandages. "What did they do to me?"

"Back up a step. Schaer clipped you in the neck but didn't hit nothing but meat. No damage to your carotid arteries or jugular veins or your spinal cord or throat or any important nerves. Just skin and meat, the doctor said. Lucky you have some extra fat protecting you."

"That ain't fucking funny," said Sal and he felt

himself being covered with the morphine mist again, but he was still conscious. "How long am I gonna be here? Have you told Lois about this?"

"Got you covered. You will be out tomorrow or, more likely, on Wednesday. I let Lois know and she is heading this direction right now. Should be here in a couple of hours. She wasn't able to reach Matt but left a message with his girlfriend."

"Matt don't give a shit. We hardly talk anymore," Sal said, speaking of his strained relationship with his only son.

"You get some rest. You bled like a stuck pig but they're pumping fresh into you now. They sucked a pint of my finest and it looks like we will actually be blood brothers. Hope you take on some of my superior traits. Don't worry. Just rest and I'll be back in the morning."

Vacek was assigned chauffeur duty and he waited for Doc in the hall. Before the visit to the hospital, they had returned to the crime scene, and they allowed Doc to retrieve his and Sal's baggage from the van. After leaving the hospital, he gave Doc a lift back to the Riverview and waited in his squad car in the motel lot. Hillman didn't want anything strange to happen to Doc until he had the chance to discuss next steps with the county attorney.

The motel phone rang at 10:00pm. "Doc, I just left Sally's bedside. Oh, my God! How do you two get into these messes? Dammit! He was talkative until he punched the little button to his drugs and then he just kind of went back to sleep. Can I come by? I don't have any place to stay."

"Lois, calm down. He's gonna be fine. Just pain and a lot of blood. Look, get somebody to tell you how to get to the Riverview Motel. I'm in room 24 this time. We got stuck here . . . anyway, I'll tell you all about it. Crazy four days."

"Don't go no place. I'll get there quick as I can. Can

you see if they have a room available?"

"I'll do that," said Doc and hung up the phone.

He walked out and noticed Vacek watching his every step from the patrol car. He rang the night bell at the motel office and the proprietor opened the door, curry wafting out of the office. As usual, there were plenty of rooms available and Doc rented 26 for Lois and paid the fee. He asked if anyplace in town delivered food that time of night. He had not eaten since early morning. There was a little pizza place that usually closed at 10 but Doc called, and a grumpy teenager answered. Doc offered a $20 tip and the kid agreed to fix a sweep-the-kitchen pie and deliver it to the motel.

Lois and the pizza arrived at the same time. Doc and Sal's wife were hugging below the walkway light when the kid walked up with the pie. He gave Doc and Lois what he thought was a knowing look. "Big night, aye sir?" the kid said and gave Doc a wink. Doc ignored the kid and took Lois and the pizza into his room. He had hit the Coke machine when he paid for Lois' room. He opened them both a Dr Pepper and sat the pizza box in the center of the little table.

Lois was much as she had always been. Short, blond, and fully packed without being fat. She had gained a few pounds since her days as a biker chick, back in Sanctuary, but she didn't look bad for woman in her late 40s. She and Doc had enjoyed a night together before she and Sal were serious. It was during one of the times when Doc and the woman he loved, Kay, were going through difficult times. Doc had also enjoyed the company of Lois' sister, who was her cookie cutter copy. There remained a sexual tension between them, but Doc had never allowed a liaison with Lois, after she and Sal had become a couple. She had always remained open to the opportunity and Sal would have had no issue with it. Such was the nature of his relationship with both Doc and Lois. There were lines Doc would not cross.

Lois lifted a wedge of pizza to her mouth and, before biting, asked, "So Doc, what the fuck happened to Sally? I have only heard bits and pieces. He was groggy when I was with him." And she inserted the point and bit off a mouthful.

Doc started with, "There was some of it I didn't see because I was being held in the living room. Obviously, Sal killed the Mexican guy with a toilet lid, but I didn't see or even hear any of that." He went on to, once again, relate the same story he had now told four times. Lois grazed through three big slices, earnestly listing as Doc spoke.

When he finished, she asked, "Are y'all in trouble? I mean two men died. What happens now?"

"Damn good question. I'm kinda worried about that, myself. The Sheriff said something about a meeting with the DA, or whoever, tomorrow. I'm wondering if I need a lawyer or if Sal does, since he was the one who killed the two men. He may need one or, maybe we both will. Hell, I just don't know but I'm supposed to be at the Sheriff's Office in the morning. I don't think the cops know what to do next because none of them have seen anything like this before. The state folks will probably take the lead, I think."

They talked a while longer and Doc ate some of the now-cold pizza. When Doc walked Lois to her room, he noticed two TV crew vans parked across the street from the motel entry. Camera men and reporters were leaning against the vehicles and came to full attention when Doc opened his door. They started in his direction, but he quickly closed Lois' door and retreated into his own room before the press was half way across the parking lot. He cleaned up the pizza and pop mess, brushed his teeth and set the clock radio for a 6:00am wake-up.

***

11.

When Doc opened his door at 6:30, the contingent of newsmen had grown. He knocked on Lois' door and she was still in a Willie Nelson T-shirt and panties, her short blond hair sticking in every direction. "What?!" she said.

"Lois, you need to get yourself together. Get you some breakfast—there's a truck stop café just down the street. Then go to the hospital until you hear from me. Got it?"

"Got it!" and she slammed her door.

Vacek had been replaced by Johnny Lopez. When he saw Doc by his door, he pulled his cruiser right up to room 24 and motioned Doc to get in. "Good morning, Mr. Quinn. You need to come with me."

"OK, Johnny. What can you tell me this morning? What kind of story did the women tell you? Anything more on Sal's condition?"

"They say he's going to be fine. Just a nice scar on his neck. Now both of you got visible scars," said the deputy, with a chuckle. Doc had a very prominent scar above his right eye, the result of a shooting that happened at the Thursday's Children MC biker bar. Doc hadn't taken a bullet, just the fragments of a man's skull exploding right in front of him from a 12-gauge blast. Lopez continued, "Must have hurt Mr. Lombardo like hell and he bled a bunch. Sheriff Hillman said that I can't discuss anything about the case with you. I have to take you to the office. There are already a bunch of people there. Folks been there all night but some from Austin came in real early this morning."

The parking area of the Sheriff's Office building was

packed with official-looking vehicles and there were more media vans across the street and filling the curbside spaces at the Fayette County Courthouse. Lopez left his cruiser running, got out and walked around and opened Doc's door and motioned him into the office. Deputy Hlavinka was at the desk, but she didn't speak, just pointed toward the conference room, with a very serious look on her face.

The conference table was filled, except for one chair. There were other folding chairs lining the wall and people were standing and sitting talking and every eye went to Doc when he walked in. He recognized Hillman, Dr. Spears, Naiser, Ranger Stafford, and the AG representative, Ryley. Doc thought He had never seen the six other men. He thought *Damn! Even more cops?*

Naiser spoke, "Mr. Quinn, take that seat and everybody settle down and we can get to the business at hand." The conversation in the room silenced and Doc sat.

Sheriff Hillman still looked distraught and very unhappy as he scanned the group gathered in his offices. It appeared he hadn't slept. With good reason, Doc thought. Hillman said, "Doc, I know you have been over this several times but some of these folks haven't heard your story before, so you are going to need to tell it again. We will be recording it and comparing the recording with the other two you made—just for comparison to see if you are consistent.

"Alright, I can do that, but I have some questions of my own and I'd like some answers."

The AGR guy, Ryley, said, "We can address your questions later. Go ahead and tell us what happened yesterday."

Doc spent the next half-hour going back over the events in as much detail as he could muster. Nobody interrupted him. When he was done, he just looked around the room and he saw questions in the eyes of several men.

The first to speak was Naiser. "My biggest question is how you decided to go to the house, in the first place. It just seems pretty unlikely to me."

"Like I said, I saw the car parked there and something just clicked. It was like the picture of the car at Monument Hill just flashed back on me. I think it was just dumb luck. Or, maybe, bad luck. Wish I'd never seen it and this mess would be left up to you folks—and me and Sal would be sipping free wine someplace in the hills."

Dr. Spears spoke up, "I can confirm that Mr. Quinn seemed to have an interest in one page of the book of vehicle samples. He went back to that page three times. That page had cars with profiles like the one I saw at the impound this morning. There was a picture of a 1979 Pontiac Grand Am that looked just like the car—red strip and all. I went back this morning and checked the picture. The actual car was a 1980 model, but they looked identical."

"Still, that was a hell of a coincidence. Almost too good to believe. That kind of thing just don't happen," said Naiser.

Ranger Stafford said, "Well John, stranger things have happened. I've seen it before. Sometimes a memory will flash. Faces and the like." Dr. Spears nodded her agreement.

A man in a suit, who Doc hadn't seen before, asked, "So you two were just snooping around the house after the car drove off. How did they get the drop on you when they drove back up? Don't seem likely to me."

Doc was getting weary of the inquisition. "We didn't have a gun on us—neither one of us. Sal' .45 was in the van but we didn't bring it to the door. We were just trying to talk to somebody at the house to see if we might need to get Sheriff Hillman involved. There would have been a lot of egg on our faces if we just called the law with nothing more to go on. Hell, there could have been a dozen cars like that in Fayette County, for all we knew. And there wasn't any way to know for sure that it was the car from the park. We didn't know. Didn't even know if the car belonged there or if it was just somebody visiting. Could have been anybody." He took a deep breath and continued, "Do I need to get a lawyer involved here? Seems like some of you think we were the ones at fault."

Ryley held up his hand and said, "Look Mr. Quinn! Don't get upset. Nobody's been arrested and I don't think that will be necessary if everything you and Mr. Lombardo tell us checks out. No need to start talking lawyers at this point. You are giving your statement of your own free will. At this point y'all are the victims here—violent and lucky victims but victims, anyway. Nobody has read you your rights or anything. If that happens, then you can start thinking lawyer."

Doc took a deep breath and said, "Is there any food and coffee around this place? I haven't even had breakfast yet."

Hillman said, "Yeah, let's take a break. We have kolaches and some breakfast tacos in the kitchen. There's coffee and you can heat stuff up in the microwave. Anybody wanting to eat, go get it and we can start back up in fifteen."

Doc was the first one in the kitchen and he picked out two sausage kolaches—really just pigs-in-a-blanket but, of late, they were being called kolaches. He also grabbed a cream cheese kolache and he filled a Styrofoam cup with coffee. He heated the pastries on a paper plate and dodged the food line back into the conference room. He was getting tired of all eyes being on him. And he was more than weary of telling the story of the previous day. He had consciously tried to tell it exactly the same each time because he thought that was important—especially the part about Sal being shot and killing Bobby Schaer.

When everyone was back in place, Naiser went around the room telling those in attendance to ask any more questions they might have. There were none. Then he stepped out and asked Deputy Hlavinka to find Johnny Lopez and for them to come in the room and tell what they had learned from the three women. The female deputy had assisted with the women because Hillman felt that a woman was appropriate to be involved with other women. Johnny was there because he was the only one truly fluent in Spanish.

Hillman said to Doc, "I think you may need to go back to the break room while we hear what Deputy Lopez has to say." Doc did as asked.

Then Lopez spoke. The story the women had told him was one of cruelty and depravity. They had all been brought across the border with promises of good jobs and to flee their whorehouse existence. It didn't turn out that way. The women—even the old lady—had been forced to perform any sexual act their captors could conjure up.

They were taught to cut and weigh the heroin and to bag it in single dose, eighth-ounce, one ounce and quarter-pound packages. The more attractive of the young women, Maria, admitted that both she and Victoria were heroin addicts and Santos would inject them as compensation when he demanded sex. They said they knew Santos, Schaer and two other men but they had overheard other men in the front of the house, from time to time, but had never seen them. They said the two other regulars spoke only broken English. They were called Ruiz and Paco. They said the only time they heard the phone ring was about two hours before the unseen men arrived. Each time the phantoms came and went, there was either a new supply of heroin or the drugs they had processed were removed from the house.

They also said that the dead girl, Victoria, or Maria would be cleaned up, dressed in a fresh shift dress, blindfolded, and taken, by Santos, to houses where men and women had used them for sex. They said that happened about once a week. Maria said it was a relief to get away from the house where they were forced to live. She said the places they were taken were nice but dark and they couldn't identify any of the people involved. Hlavinka didn't speak but stood to Lopez' side and nodded occasionally as he related the women's tale.

Those in the room questioned Lopez and Hlavinka but nothing of consequence came of it. Afterward, the meeting broke up, Doc walked out of the break room and approached Hillman, who was standing with Naiser, the AG guy, Ryley, and two others. "Sheriff, can you let me have Sal's van, so I have a way to get around? I need to go check on him. His wife came in last night and she's at the hospital now."

The men looked at each other and Naiser answered, "My men have taken about a thousand pictures and searched every inch of the damn thing. I don't see any reason to keep it impounded. Sheriff?"

Hillman said, "That's fine with me. We drove it to a wrecking yard we use as an impound. I'll get Lopez to give you a lift. But hey, you can't be leaving town until we tell you it's OK. We still need to talk to the county attorney to see if he thinks a grand jury is needed for you two. He's in court today."

"I'm not going anywhere. At least, until Sal is released from the hospital. Where am I going to go?"

"OK, me and some of these men have to give a press conference later this morning so I don't need you under foot. Go ahead and get out of here."

Doc found Lopez and they exited a side door, to

avoid the TV cameras. The deputy took him to the junk yard they used by the county as an impound. Doc asked Lopez what he had learned from the women and the Deputy gave him a condensed version, with more details than he probably should have. Lopez liked Doc a lot more than most of the men who had listened to him in the conference room. Doc picked up Sal's van and drove straight to the hospital.

***

Doc hustled down the hall to Sal's room and was happily surprised to see the big man sitting in the recliner with no tubes running into his body. His neck was heavily bandaged, and it looked fresh, with no seepage of blood.

"Well! Happy to see you sitting up. Last night I didn't know if I would ever see that again. How are you feeling?"

"Shit! The last twenty-four hours has been a blur. The morphine is almost wore off, and I'm starting to hurt some. Not so bad—I've hurt worse. They promised me some good drugs to take home. I was wondering if they put you in jail. What's been happening?"

"Hoping we can avoid jail or a trial or anything like that. No final decision on next steps. Hillman's supposed to talk to the county attorney and I don't know what the state may do. I did hear a guy—didn't catch his name—saying we were lucky ol' Schaer didn't have a wife or anything, who might sue us. Sue you, gun slinger."

"Fuck you, Doc! If I hadn't taken the bastard out, we'd both would have been goners. You know, I never liked the little asshole. I ain't sorry one bit that I blew him away. Not gonna lose any sleep over that."

"What the hell happened back in that bathroom. I never got the chance to ask last night. The state guys said you bashed Santos' head in with the back of the commode."

"He got too close. When he did, he was fucked. I butted the shit out of him but didn't knock him out. Wrapped a towel around his face to keep him quiet and then swatted him with the toilet lid. It makes a pretty grim weapon."

"Well, whatever happened, I'm glad it did."

Lois said, "You two sound like you're telling war stories. I'm just glad you ain't both dead. We can figure out the legal shit as it comes along."

They talked for several more minutes and then Hillman, Naiser and the AG rep came in and told Doc and Lois to leave the room while they interviewed Sal. They had a tape recorder and put it on the rolling bedtable and pushed it to where Sal was sitting.

"Let's get some lunch, Lois. Did you get breakfast like I told you?" asked Doc.

She didn't eat earlier so they walked downstairs to the little hospital lunch room and grabbed pre-made sandwiches, chips, and Dr Peppers. They sat at a table by a window and talked. "What did Sally tell you?" Doc asked.

"He said he didn't remember much after the shooting. He said the noise stunned him more than getting hit. Said he couldn't hear nothin'. Said you were talking to him but he didn't understand anything. Said he was in and out after that. People don't need to test him when it comes to shootin'. He's the best. Always has been, long as I known him. He's gonna be OK, ain't he?"

Doc put his hand on her shoulder and said, "Sal is the toughest son-of-a-bitch I ever knew. He's going to be just fine. He'll be proud of the scar and show it off at every opportunity. He will make up a story even better than the real thing and tell it to anybody who will put a Bud in front of him."

Lois laughed but there were tears in her eyes. "Doc,

we been together so long that I don't think I could make it without him. He's a pain in the ass but I love him."

"I know you do, baby. So do I."

***

Hillman found Doc and Lois in the lunchroom after the interview with Sal. He walked to their table and said, "We set a meeting with the County Attorney and the District Attorney at four, this afternoon. You need to find the DA's office in the Courthouse and be there to talk. See you then."

Doc just nodded his agreement and Hillman was gone. After the Sheriff made his exit, Doc said, "Lois, are you going to be OK? I'll pay for your room for another night and, then we can play it by ear."

"That's good. I told my boss at Walmart that I would be back when I got back and if that didn't suit him, he could go to hell," said Lois, and she was serious. Jobs were easier to come by than husbands. She had driven her POS '91 Dodge Daytona from Deer Park. It looked like hell, but Doc knew Sal always kept it in solid running condition, so he didn't have to worry about her getting around.

They went back up to Sal's room as an orderly was taking away his empty lunch tray. "I can't be here too long. Goddamn food ain't edible. Next time you come, can you bring me a brisket sandwich or something?"

"Well, if you are feeling well enough to bitch about the groceries, I guess you won't be in here long. I have to meet with the DA and County Attorney later. Maybe I'll find out if they plan to bring any kind of charges against us," said Doc. Then he asked, "How did the interview go with the law men?"

"Told them the truth. Just like it happened. No reason to make anything up. The truth was fucked up enough."

Then Doc leaned close to Sal's ear and said, "What happened to that bag of smoke and the X you had? We don't want to get caught with that."

"It was in my duffle in the van. What happened to my stuff?"

Doc sighed in relief. "They let me take our baggage back to the motel before they started tearing the van apart and taking their pictures. It's in room 24 at the Riverview."

"They tore the van apart! What the fuck?"

"Settle down! Not really tore anything up. I'm driving it now. They just searched it and took a shitload of pictures. It's OK. I need to call my office and let them know I might be delayed in coming back. No problem because I booked all week as vacation. I'm gonna leave y'all and I'll be back after the lawyer meeting. Hope I don't come back to see you handcuffed to the bed rail. Don't piss nobody off." He hugged Sal and Lois and walked out and down to the van.

Doc went back to the motel and just tried to chill until time to meet at the courthouse. He fell asleep sitting in the straight chair at the little round table and only awoke at a quarter-to-four. He rushed to brush his teeth, wash his face, and drove the few blocks. He was five minutes late and the lawyers, Hillman, Naiser, and Stafford glared at him.

Naiser said, "We were about to send out a search party for you. Sit down and let's talk."

Doc was surprised that the District Attorney was a woman, Madilyn Bartos. "Sorry, folks. I just nodded off for a few minutes. Been a long couple of days. Ask away—or tell me what comes next."

Bartos spoke, "Mr. Quinn, we have been reviewing this matter for the past half-hour. Mr. Schuler, he's the County Attorney—don't believe you have met before—anyway, I think we agree that there will be no charges filed against you and Mr. Lombardo at this time. No grand jury. It appears that you two were victims in this matter. We believe that Mr. Lombardo was forced to take the action he did in order to save his life and yours."

There was quiet in the room for a moment and Doc saw Hillman looking at his hands with a slight shake of his head. The Sheriff was still obviously distressed. Who wouldn't be?

Then Bartos continued, "There is a high likelihood that you two will be asked to come back and testify, presuming arrests are made in this matter. If we are able to find and arrest the others involved in this drug and hostage mess. Right now, we don't know a lot. And we really cannot tell you everything involved in the ongoing investigation. I will tell you that we have a tap on the phone and surveillance on the house. We are trying to get records of incoming and outgoing calls but that will take a while. Maybe it will lead us someplace.

"We have also taken finger prints from the house and the drug packages there. We will need to get yours and those of Mr. Lombardo to eliminate you as suspects.

"Since the women were taken from a brothel across the border, the likelihood of learning anything meaningful there is nil. And, we have no way to trace the sex trafficking angle, here locally. The women don't know or are unwilling to give us anything. They just want to get back across the border but the younger one said she'd love to go home with you and be your housekeeper." The men chuckled.

There was another pause with the attendees looking at one another without comment. The DA was obviously the person in charge at this meeting and the reactions of some, including Hillman and, especially Ryley, made it clear to Doc that they were less than comfortable with her leading the discussions. It would have been easy for them to feel that she was sharing too much information.

She continued, "With the only two known offenders being dead and neither having a known spouse, it's difficult to know who to talk to next. The other man didn't even have ID on him or in his car. We are running his vehicle, but first indication is that it was stolen in San Antonio two years ago and it had stolen plates, as well. Unless we can get some evidence on the drug operation, we are limited to prosecute. Since the media is blowing up on this thing, the other parties involved are probably aware of what went down. Unless they are just stupid, they're putting some distance between themselves and Fayette County.

"The important thing for you and Mr. Lombardo is that you will be free to go but we will need every bit of contact information for you both because we will surely have occasion to bring you back here sometime in the future. We would appreciate it if neither of you talk about this matter with the press or even with your families and friends. Again, I remind you that the investigation is ongoing and will be for some time.

"Do you have any questions? If not, you will follow Sheriff Hillman back to his office to be fingerprinted and to leave your contact info with him. Mr. Lombardo will be fingerprinted at the hospital before he is dismissed." As an afterthought she said, "Oh, we will have to hold Mr. Lombardo's pistol as evidence. At least for a while."

Doc considered what he heard and said, "I don't think I have any questions. I'll be here until Sal is released from the hospital, but I'll let the Sheriff know when we leave town."

What she didn't share was that the state police were checking Bobby Schaer's home and bank records for a money trail. In the end, they found the money but there was no trail. With Sheriff Hillman's help, they located over $10,000 in cash and gold coins in Schaer's house and a like amount of money tucked away in a Columbus bank account he had established over a year earlier. This indicated his involvement in the drug operation went back at least that long. Hillman wondered how he could have been so blind as not to have known there was a problem with his brother-in-law.

With that, the meeting ended and everyone went on their respective ways. Doc was finger printed and then returned to the hospital. He found Sal scraping at a slice of dry turkey with a plastic knife. "Did you bring me that barbeque I asked for? This shit's hard to stomach." Lois was sitting on the bed and just shook her head.

"Sorry, brother. I plumb forgot. The good news is that we are free to haul ass as soon as they turn you loose. They need to fingerprint you and hold your pistol for a while. I imagine you will hear from them first thing in the morning."

They sat and talked for a while. Doc gave Sal a recap of all the DA had said. He stayed until the nurse came and told them visiting hours were over. Sal cursed but the nurse had heard it all before.

Doc and Lois returned to the Riverview for the evening. Doc slept hard for eight hours and then went to the truck stop café and picked up sausage and egg biscuits for breakfast for Lois and himself. Lois picked up a change of clothes from Sal's duffle and they checked out of the motel. By the time they reached the hospital, Deputy Hlavinka had just finished with the fingerprinting. Sal was checked out of the hospital and took the mandatory wheelchair ride to the sliding door exit. He rode with Lois in her Dodge and Doc followed in the van as they returned to Deer Park.

Lois insisted on fetching barbeque and for Doc to eat and spend the night. That was fine with him. The next morning, Doc transferred his belongings to his Tahoe and was ready to head back to San Antonio. When Doc looked at his pristine SUV, he was glad Sal had convinced him to use the van for their getaway.

Standing beside Doc's ride, Sal said, "You know, I'm really bummed about the damage to my van. I joked about it being a classic. We all know it was an old piece of shit, but I love the damn thing. Only carry the required liability insurance so getting it fixed up may take a while."

"If you need some help getting it repaired, just let me know. As it is, it will get lots of attention and you can tell some stories. Or, hell, you could duct tape up the holes and park it in your back yard. Just go out and sit in it and smoke a number once in a while," said Doc.

"Don't be an asshole. I start a new gig next week. Out on the Ship Channel, doing some piping design work. Should last about four months. I'll be OK. What do you think will happen about that shit in LaGrange?"

"Man, I am clueless. I don't see how they can get to the bottom of the smack thing. I mean, you killed their only two real connections. Ain't nobody gonna call or come to the house. The fucking TV people took care of that. Things in LaGrange will probably settle back to whatever is normal there. I feel bad for Sheriff Hillman. He's not a bad guy and he means well. Having old Schaer on his payroll won't help him, come reelection time. He'll probably be OK, I guess."

Sal thought for a bit and said, "Do you suppose Darling had anything to do with anything?"

"I can't imagine how. I mean, his clubhouse, or whatever it is, would have been the perfect place for the women and heroin operation but I think he's just a bored rich guy. Probably never hear of him or his wife again. I gotta be hitting the road. Love you brother. Talk to you soon."

The men bearhugged and Doc drove away. From Sal's house to Doc's condo was 224 miles and Doc fought the midday traffic through Houston and on down I-10 to San Antonio. He got back home after 4:00pm.

Doc had learned to live alone many years before, but walking into his empty home always made the loneliness descend on him like a heavy blanket. He turned his AC down to 72 and flopped on his couch, hoping for a nap. He closed his eyes but pictures from the past week flashed through his mind. Finally, he gave up and ordered a pizza for delivery.

***

12.

Doc woke up late on Friday morning—a few minutes after six. Unusual for him. His first thought was to call his office, but he got over it. He found his despised pager and there were two messages, but he ignored them. He unplugged his cell phone from the charger and found several missed calls. They were all from his office on Wednesday and Thursday. Evidently, after people there heard of the events in LaGrange. He hadn't considered it before but now realized that his name had probably appeared in the San Antonio newspaper, as it had in Austin. He hadn't seen any TV reports on the matter, and he had no idea that his name had been given to the media and they had mentioned him as well as Sally. He decided to call his secretary at nine.

Doc had hired Sonja when he opened the San Antonio office. She was not a young woman even then and now she was nearing 70 but still dependable and with no idea of retiring. She loved Doc like a son and fussed over him like a mother hen. "Hello, Talmadge Supply," she answered the phone.

"Sonja, this is Doc. Just checking in."

"Goddamn you, Doc! Why didn't you let us know. Everybody's been worried sick, wondering what happened to you. Are you OK?" the old woman wanted to know.

"Settle down, Sonja. I'm fine. It was just a crazy couple of days. How are things going at the company?"

"Everything's fine. Now that you decided to check in. Are you coming in today?"

"I took the weeks' vacation so, no, I'm not coming in

today. Talmadge can survive without me until Monday."

"That's what I told Chicago when they called. I don't think the news made it that far north and I didn't tell them anything. When you come in on Monday, you have to tell me all about it. Must have been just awful."

"It's all just fine. Been in tougher places. I'm fine. My friend, Salvatore, is fine. Don't worry about me. It will all blow over and things will be back to normal by Monday. I'm just gonna lay low and decompress for the weekend. If there is an emergency, give me a call on the cellular or just call my house number. I'm not planning to go out, except maybe for a steak or something."

When the call ended, Doc laid back on his couch and turned the TV to CNN to catch up on the news, but he quickly tired of the headlines. The only thing that was of interest was an agreement between Venezuela and the US which might—or might not—impact the price of oil. His company had been hoping to expand further into South America and this might be important. Not important enough to keep him from napping through most of the morning. He tried to go to the gym that afternoon but his effort to work out was half-hearted, so he gave up after a half-hour of stretching and working the Nautilus machines. The weekend's only activity was making the short drive to Helotes for that steak at his favorite, the Grey Moss Inn. When he got home, there was a message on his answering machine from one of the two women he had been seeing. He ignored it.

When he arrived at the office on Monday morning, Sonja greeted him at the door and wrapped him in a perfume and powder embrace. All fourteen of his local employees had gathered in the break room and wanted to hear Doc's story. He obliged, keeping it short and simple. Just the facts as he knew them. He didn't mention being handcuffed and held at gunpoint. He told everyone he was fine and encouraged them to go back to work and make the company some money.

Doc had built an impressive career at Talmadge. He had worked for the company for twenty-seven years, in a series of increasingly important roles. He had given up his studies for a PhD and joined the company when he was twenty-five. Change was not something Doc sought out. He was more comfortable with familiarity. His intelligence and hard work had paid dividends for him. At fifty, he was Regional Vice President for his company, covering Texas and all its surrounding states with eleven offices, each with a warehouse, and service center. Talmadge was an integral part of a huge, multi-national corporation. Doc had done a two-year bit in the corporate office, located in a Chicago suburb, and had visited their subsidiaries on four continents. Ultimately, he asked to return to his old haunts and the company granted his request, with the understanding that he might be asked to return to the corporate office at some point.

He wasn't a Texas native but felt like one. He loved the state and its diverse population and geography. Living in San Antonio, he had developed an interest in state history and spent many of his weekends visiting various parks and monuments. That's how he grew to love the Monument Hill site at LaGrange.

Sal had followed Doc to Texas, first with a job working for one of Doc's client companies. The big man had put down roots in the Houston area and he stayed busy as a contract employee for numerous companies. Always a fisherman, he had become an expert in saltwater angling. He preferred fishing to working and this, along with his independent attitude, had not always served him well, professionally.

Doc's week flowed along easily, once he had told his abbreviated tale to his Chicago boss, several clients and the two women in his life. One of the women, Kathy, went to dinner with him on Friday. She was thirty-four and marketing manager for an upscale women's clothing store. She spent the night at Doc's condo. On Sunday, he had brunch with his other lady friend, Janice. She was forty-one and a middle school principal. Both women were Texans, born and bred, and both were very attractive, educated, sophisticated and interesting to be around. Doc was fond of them and enjoyed being with them but neither held an important place in Doc's heart. He loved women but would never commit to one—a circumstance which kept his relationships short and shallow. Women with long term in mind learned quickly to move on.

Two weeks following his return to San Antonio, he received a call at his office from a DCI officer, named Windell Hankins—yet another cop now involved. The list was getting long. "Mr. Quinn, we met briefly at the DA's office in LaGrange. I just wanted to follow up with you. Did you think of anything more that might give us any leads in the drug case? Or concerning the women?"

Doc had no recollection of having met Hankins, but he wanted to be cooperative. "I have thought on it quite a lot. Kept me awake at night more than once. I think we covered everything that I know. If anything had come to me, I'd have called Sheriff Hillman. Have you spoken to Sal Lombardo again? Maybe he remembered something more."

"We've spoken to him twice. We wanted to confirm some things about the death of Santos Ramos De La Garza—that was his name. He was from Tampico, but nobody there gave up any information. He may have been affiliated with a well-known bunch of drug smugglers there, but we can't confirm it. Drug gangs are a scourge in Mexico these days. Seem to be running everything in some places."

"Has there been any scuttlebutt about retribution for the man's death? I mean, we need to be prepared if anybody is looking for Sal or me."

"I don't think you need to worry too much about that. Getting killed is an occupational hazard in that line of business. I'd wager that nobody but his *mamacita* even cares he's gone."

Doc thought for a beat and said, "Well, pity the fool who tries to mess with Sal! And I stay pretty well armed myself—at least, when I'm home or if I expect trouble."

"Mr. Quinn, if those kinds of people wanted to do you harm, it would happen before you even knew it was happening. I think you are going to be OK. Oh, and I would ask that you contact Mr. Ryley if you think of anything more. I believe you have his contact information. The Sheriff has enough on his plate without being bothered by this matter any further."

"Yeah, I suppose you are right about that. I'll let him know if I think of anything." And the conversation was over. Doc didn't care for Hankins' dismissal of Sheriff Hillman, who had been the one constant throughout the events and the man that Doc trusted the most. He would contact Hillman first if there was a need. To hell with the state bureaucrats—Hillman was boots on the ground.

***

13.

Doc was at his desk on October 20 when Sonja buzzed him. "Doc, there's a lady on the phone wanting to talk to you. Says her name is Darlene Darling. What kind of bullshit is that? Anyway, do you want to talk to her?"

Doc said, "Sure. Put her through."

"What are you up to? That sounds like some sort of stripper name?" Sonja laughed as she punched off and forwarded the call to Doc.

"Hello, this is Connor Quinn."

"Well hello, handsome! I hope you are all recovered from the mess in LaGrange. This is Darlene Darling."

"This is a pleasant surprise. I'm fine. I recover quick. Especially when I don't get shot or beat up too bad. Hope everything is peaches with you."

"Peaches and cream!" she laughed. "Look, I'll be spending a few days in San Antone this week. I was hoping we might be able to have some dinner and get to know each other a little better."

"What would ol' Jack have to say about that?"

"You let me worry about *ol' Jack.* No, he's gonna be going to Dallas to spend some quality time with friends and to go to the Red River Rivalry game on Saturday—you know, Texas and Oklahoma. So, I'm on my own for a few days. Like I told you before, Jack does his thing and I do mine. How 'bout some dinner. I'll treat."

"I think I'd enjoy that. But you will never buy me dinner. Ladies don't buy in my world."

"Oh my God! A gentleman on top of it all. I don't care who picks up the check. I'll hit town on Thursday. I believe I told you we keep a time share on the River Walk and I'll be staying there. Meet me at the Palacio Del Rio's bar on Thursday at eight. We'll grab some dinner and talk. Will that work for you?"

"Sounds good. I'll be there."

"I'll be there waiting! My place is only a couple of blocks away and I know a good little cafe for dinner. Be there, big boy." And she hung up.

For the next three days, Doc wondered if he should have just discouraged the meeting. But he found Darlene Darling very interesting. This was a woman who was beautiful, wealthy, enjoyed the touch of a man, shot like a pro, was married but independent, and had expressed interest in him. What more could an unattached man ask for? He wanted to find out. Maybe it was just dinner. Maybe something more. He told Sonja he might take a half-days' vacation on Friday. Maybe the whole day. She rolled her eyes and breathed a heavy sigh but didn't say anything.

***

The Thursday weather was still Texas autumn—warm but not uncomfortably hot—so, after work, he showered, shaved again, put on tan slacks, an off-white Cinch shirt, his cocoa-colored Lucchese boots with a matching, silver-appointed gentleman's belt. He wore a lightweight, nubby silk, brown sports jacket, and no tie. When he looked at himself in the mirror, he thought that it wasn't great but was about as good as it was likely to get. He couldn't remember when he was quite this nervous for a date—and he had been on a *lot* of dates over the past quarter-century.

Doc parked his Tahoe with the valet at the Palacio Del Rio and found his way to the bar. He was ten minutes early and stood at the side of the doorway and saw her immediately. He had always liked to see people before they saw him—especially women. He liked to watch what they were doing before he arrived. She was sitting at the bar, which was almost empty. She was talking to the bartender with a martini glass in front of her. There were two olives on the little sword, and she was stirring it around in the dingy liquid. Doc knew this was what was called a 'dirty' martini, although he had never tasted one.

She leaned forward, one elbow on the bar rail and the bartender craned across the bar to be as close to her as possible. Maybe she was talking low. Maybe he was checking out her cleavage. Or maybe he was a normal man, wishing to be as close to beauty as possible. And she was beautiful on this night. Even more so than he had realized before. Her long golden hair was perfectly swept over her right shoulder, like pictures he had seen of Veronica Lake. Her face looked untouched, but he knew that was the effect she was going for. Around her neck was diamond drop and her fingers were adorned with the same jewels he had seen at the SPJST dance. She wore a low-cut, straight, blue, shiny dress, split to mid-thigh, above stilettos of the same blue. Her legs were tanned, bare and crossed as she sat half-sideways to her barstool.

A man in an expensive suit, his tie loosened, strolled up to her side and that was Doc's cue to join her. He overheard her tell the man, "I have a drink, thank you very much." Then she saw Doc advancing and went on, "I'm waiting for someone and here he comes." The man looked back at Doc, nodded, and walked back to the table he shared with two other suits who had a laugh at their friend's expense.

"About damn time you showed up! I was liable to get a better offer," she said, with a broad smile. She wrapped her arms around Doc when he got to her side. She smelled amazing and she hugged with some enthusiasm. Then she leaned back and said, "What are you drinking?

I'm just finishing this, but you can buy me another." And she took the remains of her martini in a single swallow.

"I'll have a Glenlivet 18 and whatever the lady is having. You can start a tab," he said to the bartender, who looked a bit crestfallen at Doc's arrival. To Darlene, he said, "You look magnificent! It's great to see you."

"Let's get a table. You don't look so bad your damn self," she said as she grabbed Doc's hand and led him to a corner table. He pulled her chair out and she sat, crossing her legs and looking intently into Doc's face. The bartender delivered their drinks and went away.

"So, Jack's gone to Dallas to watch football?"

"Let's get him out of the way. I told you that he does his thing and I do mine and, sometimes, we do some things together. We love each other but we understand each other. Space makes our kind of marriage work. Not for everybody but works for us. Have you ever been married. Can't imagine a catch like you has been on your own for life. Of course you have!"

"Don't know about the *catch* thing but, yes, I was married twice. Once when I was just a stupid kid in college. That wasn't meant to last. My second wife . . . she was killed in a motorcycle wreck."

"How long have you been single?"

"That was twenty-three years ago. Never found a reason to get married again."

She looked deeply into his eyes for a long moment and pursed her lips. "There has to be a story there. I can tell by the way your face changed when you talk about her."

"Probably. But it's not a story for here or now. Let's just enjoy our evening. Is that OK?"

"Damn! A man of mystery. I'll let it drop now but, eventually, I'll soften you up and you'll tell me all the juicy details."

They drank in silence for several minutes. Both

pretended to take in the sights in the bar and the crowds passing on the River Walk. Then Doc said, "So you have a place near here? The River Walk is best in the winter, late at night. When the lights are all still in the cypress trees but the crowds have gone home for the night."

"I know! I love it then. Between Christmas and New Year. How long have you been living here?"

"Off and on for over twenty years. Oh, I did a two-year bit in my corporate office in Chicago, but I guess this, or the town where I used to live . . . well, one or the other is home. Somehow, this doesn't seem like home. Neither does Sanctuary—where I lived several years before coming here. Do you know what I mean? Never have felt like I was at home, anywhere. Does that make sense?"

"Not only good looking and mysterious but deep! You may have it all," she said and couldn't keep from laughing at herself.

They finished their drinks and ordered another. When that drink arrived, Doc said, "Where is that place you like to eat? Thought I knew just about every place on the Walk."

"It's just a little place, one story above the walk, itself. It's called Piro's. I'll show you. Drink up and we can go. I called ahead and they will have a table for us."

The walk was not a short one, as the River Walk promenades go. Doc walked between the water and Darlene—the gentlemanly thing to do. She hooked her left arm into his right, and they dodged tourists and, ten minutes later, she pointed to a staircase to a door with an unassuming little sign that just said *Piro's*. When they entered the small room with only six tables, a short, rotund woman greeted them. "Miss Darlene! So glad to have you back with us. Your table is ready." And she led them to a table for two, next to a window, with a view down on the bustle of the River Walk. She ordered another dirty martini and Doc had another Scotch—a 12-year-old Macallan, this time.

"I hope you don't want to eat heavy tonight. I find being too full takes away from the evening," she said.

Doc thought he understood her comment but couldn't be sure. He didn't know her well enough yet. "I'm not too hungry and wouldn't want it to get in the way of this fine whisky."

She gave him a knowing look and just smiled. They had small house salads and ordered six-ounce filets—very rare—with only bread on the side. Doc had wondered about her background. All he knew was that she was strikingly beautiful, married to a rich man, and could handle a shotgun better than most experts. "We have talked a bit about my past, but you haven't shared anything with me. Where did you grow up?"

She mostly pushed her food around on the plate and ate little. After a moment, she said, "Oh, that's so boring, isn't it. I'm sure your past is a lot more interesting than mine."

"Not at all! You intrigue me. You are not an average woman, whatever that means."

"Well, OK. I was raised in Tyler and went to Kilgore JC, first. I was a Rangerette. Can you believe that?"

"I can certainly believe that! I doubt there were many who looked like you in that lineup."

"You'd be surprised. Well, I got my business degree from Baylor and was lucky enough to get a job in real estate—commercial real estate—in Dallas. When I was twenty-three, friends wanted me to try out for the Cowboys cheerleader thing. I went to one practice and said 'fuck it' because I thought it was too much like the whole beauty pageant scene. Plus, it was like a full-time job. I had a job."

"Where did you meet Jack? Dallas?"

"Yeah, he was just getting started. He was fifteen

years older than me, but he was pretty and treated me nice."

"I guess he came from money?"

"Hardly! He grew up in the lower middle class but wanted more. Went to UT on scholarships. He made his start because he inherited some prime land from his grandfather. It was right where they wanted to build a big, new mall on the north side of Dallas. That's when I met him. He made a ton of money from that, met some of the right people and used them to make some very lucrative investments with the money from the land. For ten years, everything he touched turned to gold. Not from any superior intelligence on his part. Mostly dumb luck but I'd rather be lucky than smart," she said and laughed.

They finished their steak and ordered espresso, which came in tiny cups with tiny spoons, a twist of lemon peel and a sugar cube. She used neither and quaffed the dark liquid in one swallow. Doc opted for the sugar cube in his. Then she said, "Let me show you my place. I think you will like it." She was smiling broadly, and no man could have resisted.

"I'll get the check and we can walk over." He motioned to the waiter and used his platinum FedEx to pay.

***

"It's not far," she said, and they walked down the stairs and back onto the River Walk. Just fifty yards further she motioned to another set of steps, and they went up two flights. She punched in a code and opened the door. The place was like something from a copy of 'Architectural Digest'—modern but classic at the same time. Every detail was planned and executed by professionals.

"This is quite the apartment! You say it's a time

share? Looks too personal for that."

"Well, maybe it's not like a normal timeshare. No 'two weeks a year' limitations. We own it with Steve McDole and his wife. It's empty most of the time but it gives me a place to get away when things get too boring in LaGrange. Let me show you around."

They walked through the place. Two bedrooms, two bathrooms, a small kitchen, wet bar and the parlor—every detail was upscale and meticulously planned. The last room he saw was the master bedroom with its California king bed. "Why don't you fix us a drink. There is a bottle of Stoli and a bottle of Don Julio in the freezer. I'll have vodka. You can have whatever you want. The bar is stocked. I'll get comfortable and find something to make us feel even better," she said.

Doc had no idea what the *something* might be, but he wasn't adverse to a little smoke to take the edge off. He fixed himself a Macallan 18 on ice and took the frosty bottle of vodka out of the freezer and sat a crystal shot glass beside the bottle, wanting it to be superbly icy when she returned. But she didn't return.

Five minutes later, he heard her call out from the master bathroom, "Doc, why don't you bring me my drink in the bathroom? We can have a little something else after I do my shot."

Doc poured the ropy vodka into the shot glass, put the bottle back in the freezer and took the drinks into the master bath. Darlene Darling was standing in front of the mirror, brushing her long hair out. She glanced at him in the mirror and smiled. She had changed into a short black gown and it appeared there was nothing but her beneath the fine, thin silk. She pointed to a settee against the wall, next to the walk-in shower. "Sit down and take a load off. You may need to conserve your strength," she said and chuckled. He sat. She shot the vodka in one gulp and handed him an expertly rolled joint and silver lighter. He lit up and took a deep drag. It was excellent pot.

She was busy at the counter. She took a little glassine bag from a drawer along with a straw and square of foil. She tapped just a bit of a brown, oily-looking powder on the foil and reached back to Doc for the lighter. She held the lighter under the foil until the powder smoked, dropped the lighter and used the straw to suck the smoke into her lungs. She put down the straw and foil and rolled her head with her eyes closed with a languid smile on her face. Doc had heard of this approach but had never seen it before.

"Would you like some of this? It's nice," she said, as she looked sleepily into Doc's eyes.

"I think I'm fine with the grass and Scotch. Never have done any of that. How does it make you feel?"

"Like . . . it's amazing. Don't do it much. Just when things are . . . special. Are things going to be special?"

"It's already special for me."

"Get me another Stoli and join me in the bedroom."

Doc did as she directed. When he got to the bedroom, she was lying across the sheets on the big bed. Her gown had pushed up so he could see her magnificent legs but not higher. She raised on one elbow, just enough to take the shot glass and empty it. She held out her hand for the joint, which Doc was still carrying. He traded the empty glass for the pot. She took a hit and handed it back to him and said, "Get comfortable, big guy. Let's get a little crazy."

He thought he had left crazy in the rear-view mirror the moment he walked into the apartment. He put what was left of the joint in an ashtray on the bedside table. He removed his boots, took off his clothes, and laid down beside her. Her eyes were closed now but she had a smile on her face. He cradled her head and they kissed for the first time. It struck him as unusual that they were lying in a bed, about to have sex and this was their first kiss. It was an amazing kiss. Then she rolled away just enough to slip out of her gown. When she rolled back to his side, her hand went directly to his manhood and she said, "Well, hello there!"

Doc said, "Darlene, I'm fifty years old so you don't need to expect too much. I'm not the man I once was." He was only half kidding. She laughed and kissed him again without taking her hand away.

As his hands and mouth discovered her body, he realized that she might have been the most impressive specimen of womanhood he had ever known. Every inch of her was soft and smooth, yet firm and toned. There were no scars. She had never needed the knife to enhance what nature had given her. She had never experienced childbirth or felt mistreatment—at least, none that had left lasting marks. Her pubic hair was trimmed close and soft, and she was moist and responded to his touch. Doc had wondered if the skag would limit a woman's ability to feel and enjoy—with her, at least, it seemed to have no deleterious effects.

When he bent to that place between her legs, she took his hair in her hands and pulled him closer. As he worked, she said, "Bite it! Bite it. Please!" And he nipped at her clitoris and she pushed hard against his lips and front teeth and moved her hips to the rhythm of his tongue and hand. It took only a few minutes before she shivered, groaned, and pushed his head back. "Enough! I can't take it!" They both laughed as he pushed up to his elbows and she closed her knees tight together and wriggled.

"My God Doc! Where did you learn that? Give me a minute and I'm gonna fuck your eyes out. I want a cigarette!"

Doc stood up and found his jacket and took out his pack of Marlboros. He took the ashtray from the bedside table and placed it between them as they lay across the width of the bed. He placed one in her lips and held the lighter for her and then lit his own. "I hope that was OK."

"OK, hell! I could get used to that. You have no idea how many men don't have a clue when they are eye-to-eye with the little man in the boat." And she laughed. When she finished half of her cigarette, she scooted off the bed and said, "Don't go away. I'll be back." And she disappeared into the bathroom. Doc thought he heard the rustle of her foil and the strike of the lighter. When she came back into the room, her blue eyes looked even more dreamy than before, their lids half closed. She stood by the bed for a moment, hands on her perfect hips. "Your turn now. If you want to get a little freaky, take a look in here," and she tossed him a small tote bag that had been on the bedroom chair. Doc zipped the bag open and looked inside. There were three different kinds of vibrators, a riding crop, and two sets of handcuffs—one, a standard police issue, and the other being two little fur-padded belts with buckles, held together with a chrome chain.

"Don't know that I need to be handcuffed. Got enough of that back in LaGrange," he said with a chuckle which was lost on her. He extracted an especially unusual vibrator with an extra short, nubby arm. He hadn't seen one before but thought he understood its purpose. He turned the knob on the end, and it emitted a low buzzing and then turned it off.

"Gimme that," she said and took the bag and pulled out the riding crop and handed it to him. "You may need this!" She flopped on the bed and took the vibrator and turned it on and held it between her legs and shivered. She handed it back to him and said, "See if you can figure out what to do with this." He did.

Their love making went on for most of two hours. Each time Doc felt himself ready to explode, he pulled away and used the vibrator or his hands to stimulate her. He would change position and manipulate her body in more ways than he had done with any woman for years. She went through the motions with experience and skill. Sometimes she wanted it gentle and sometimes, rough. She picked up the riding crop, handed it to him and turned facing away from him with her beautiful backside toward him. She told him to pull her hair—hard—when he was behind, with her on hands and knees. "Use it," she said and reached back to his hand holding the whip. He smacked her buttocks and she said, "Harder!" He did and saw whelps rise on her skin and she moaned with each smack. Later they shifted again, with her on top of him, her face in his crotch and his face again against hers. And Doc knew he had never encountered a woman who could manage 69 with her expertise.

When she moved down and straddled him, it was so good that he was helpless. Finally, he said, "Don't move a muscle!" and she didn't—entirely still, internally and externally. But it felt too good and he couldn't stop. With two more thrusts, he was spent, and she felt it and rolled off and laid her head on his stomach.

"Lady, are you trying to kill me?" Doc asked with a snicker, catching his breath. "No round two. Any time soon, anyway."

"I don't think I could handle it. Even if you could. Any of that roach left?"

Doc untangled himself from her and the sheets and found the ashtray with the inch of the joint that was left. He carefully lit it and put it to her lips, and she inhaled deep and coughed hard for a moment. "Let's get something to drink and get some air on the balcony," she said and popped up and scurried into the bathroom.

Doc had the immediate and strong need to pee so he ran to the other bath and relieved himself. She was behind the bar as he walked back toward the big bedroom. She had poured him a Scotch and was pulling the vodka bottle from the freezer. She was wearing a long, terrycloth robe and she pointed to another one folded on the bar. He slipped it on, and she handed him his drink and gulped down her own. "Get the smokes and meet me on the balcony," she said.

By then, it was past two in the morning and the River Walk was deserted except for two strolling couples and a huddle of would-be gang-bangers who were afraid to make trouble because there was a cop doing the River Walk beat. The air had cooled, and they both wrapped their robes tighter. Doc leaned against the wrought iron railing and felt her hand on his.

"Tonight was great. I mean, it isn't over yet but . . . I mean, could we do it again? I'm here until Sunday. If you aren't too busy, maybe we could go to the show at the Aztec tomorrow. Texas music kind of thing. Been before. Have you?"

"If I'm able to walk again by then," he laughed. "Sounds great. And, I have been to the Aztec before but not that show. Heard about it but never went. That's how it goes. Locals never seem to do the cool stuff that attracts the tourists."

They enjoyed the cool air and smoked their cigarettes. He had seen enough of Darlene Darling that it raised more questions in his mind than it provided answers. As they stared out at the trees and water, he said, "You said earlier that you do your thing and he does his and that, sometimes, you do it together. You like a little kink in your good times. Just so I'll be better prepared, tell me a little about things that y'all do."

She was very stoned when she looked at the side of his face and said, "Oh, I see now! You like a little vicarious shit, do you? You little voyeur!" She said it with a crooked smile.

"I'm always willing to learn from the best. Hey, if you don't want to talk about it, I'm good." And he pulled her in for a kiss.

When they parted, she again had lust in her eyes. The woman was unsatiable, or that was Doc's take on her.

"Let's go back to bed and I'll tell you some stuff, if you really want to know." And she flipped her cigarette butt in the general direction of the river water. Doc did the same and they walked back to the bedroom. But there was no talk of fun and games with Jack Darling or anyone else. Their lovemaking was more passionate, slower, and without the need for toys or talk. Doc found it, somehow, more satisfying. Afterward, they both fell asleep in the damp satin sheets.

The sun coming through the sheer curtains woke him from dreamless sleep. His head was on fire with hangover. Darlene was still fast asleep, so Doc exited the bed, with as little disturbance as possible, and walked into the bathroom. He took a steaming shower and used his finger and some of her toothpaste to wash the funk from his mouth. That made him feel better, but he needed aspirins and coffee—badly. He looked around for a comb and, when he opened the top drawer of the bureau, he saw no comb but the foil square, straw, a half-empty bag of brown dope and two unopened bags. He wondered if her 'recreational' use of the drug was just her periodic escape or if she actually had an addiction. He wasn't judgmental. He had known many people over the years who depended on their habits to make it through the day. He had never been dependent on alcohol or any drug, but he thought he understood that it was human. Even good people often succumbed to the allure of feeling better with the help of substances.

He dressed in the clothes he had worn the night before because that was all he had. He sat on the side of the bed and looked at the woman who had been so animated the night before. He was amazed at how young and innocent she seemed, in her slumber. He hesitated but felt he needed to say goodbye. He gently nudged Darlene's shoulder and she slowly opened her eyes and gazed into his.

"Just leave the money on the dresser before you go," she half whispered and then she giggled. Then she reached up and pulled him down to her and hugged and kissed him on the cheek. "You don't want any tongue right now. My mouth feels like the whole Italian army slept in it." she said, still smiling.

"Gotta go. I'd like to stay but I need to touch base with my office. And I need a nap! Are we on for the Aztec tonight? I'll call you later."

"OK. Call on my cell phone." She took a note pad and pen from the drawer of the night stand and scribbled the number and poked the paper in his shirt pocket. "Now, I gotta get some serious rest. You wore me out!" They hugged again and he was gone.

Outside the air was crisp for an October morning. He tried to get his bearings and that took several seconds. Then he walked along the River Walk in the still, with only the maintenance crews clearing last night's trash. At the Palacio Del Rio he hit the gift shop for a two-pill dose of Excedrin, a fresh pack of Marlboros and a free cup of weak coffee. He drove to his condo in the midst of the early rush hour traffic and, by the time he got home, he was exhausted. He crashed on his couch and dreamed of a motorcycle ride on a country road with Kay behind him.

***

14.

When Doc woke up, it was almost 1:00pm. His headache was gone but he still felt tired. Being fifty wasn't like being twenty-five. Days following a party hurt worse than they used to. He brewed strong, dark coffee and had two cups with his instant oatmeal and toast. Then he called his office.

"Talmadge Supply. How may we help you?" It was Sonja and she sounded in a fine mood.

"It's me. Is everything running smoothly?"

"Well! I guess this means you won't be coming in today." There was a bit of practiced contempt in the old woman's voice. He knew it was for effect.

"No. I think I'll take the rest of the day as vacation. I have plenty. Anything important that I should know? And, hey! Don't judge yet ye be judged."

"Smart ass. I didn't figure you would be in today. No important calls. Guy from Enron wanted to invite you on a deer hunt next month but I told him you would get with him on Monday. No Chicago calls. A stack of mail but you can read it later. Did you have fun last night?" She said the last bit with a chuckle.

"You don't need to worry about me. I can handle it."

"OK. Enjoy your day off while the rest of us slave in your service." And she hung up.

Then he called Fat Sally, knowing his friend worked half-days on Friday. "Hello, brother. How's it hanging?"

"Don't hang—too short—just sort of bobs up and down when I walk. What's up?"

"Do you remember Darlene Darling? From

LaGrange?"

"How could somebody forget that fine thing? Sure. Did y'all hook up? Did she visit historic San Antone?"

"Spent the night with her. I'll give you the blow-by-blow when I see you, but I wanted to ask if you thought any more about her and ol' Jack since we were there. I mean, do you think they could be mixed up in that mess, somehow?"

"Shit, man. I don't know. Hadn't really considered it. Try not to think about LaGrange. Well, except when I look in the mirror and see this scar on my neck. Damn thing still hurts like hell sometimes."

"OK. She had some of that brown heroin. Had at least three of them little wax-paper-looking baggies. She smoked the stuff. Used a little sheet of foil and a straw. Never seen that done before, but then I've never been around much heroin. Even back in the old days."

"Me neither. Knew this guy at work that did something like that with crack cocaine. Guess it all works about the same. Seemed like a terrible waste of coke, but I never tried it."

"Probably a good thing crack wasn't around when we were still crazy. These days, I figure coke would blow my heart up."

"You are sure getting to be an old lady in your advanced years."

"Go to hell. Anyway, the smack looked just like the little bags we saw at the house. Gotta wonder if there's a connection. I'm seeing her again tonight and I'll try to get more information from her."

"Let me know what you find out. If there's something there, then we will have to decide if we want to tell Hillman or anybody. Never liked a rat but . . ."

"The *but* is that the motherfuckers were trying to kill us! OK. I'll fill you in later."

"And don't forget! I want to know about every inch

of that woman. She's finer than anything I've seen. If she's half as good as she looks, she'd be twice as good as anything I ever had."

After his call with Sal, he found the note in the pocket of his shirt from the night before and he called the number she had written. "Good afternoon! What are you doing with your day?" he asked when she picked it up.

"I was wondering if you would call me or just leave a girl hanging. Been a lazy day for me. I needed R&R after your rough handling last night. My butt is sore! You need to kiss it and make it well."

"I'll look forward to doing just that. Are we still on for the Aztec tonight?"

"I'm up for it if you are. Meet me outside the theater at seven. I think the doors open at half-past and the show starts at eight. You can buy tickets and we will have time for a drink before it starts."

"OK. We can get a late dinner after, or something."

"I'm thinking *or something* might be more fun. How 'bout I get us some snacks here at the apartment and we can eat a bite then?"

"Sounds like a workable plan to me. See you at seven."

***

Doc spotted Darlene a half block away. Her back was to him and the view was fantastic. She was wearing skin tight, shrink-fit Levi's, tucked inside her tall, hand-tooled boots. Her shirt was a snap-button, western cut in shiny, electric blue. Her hair was in a ponytail that went almost to her waist. He was in a blue chambre shirt, starched Wranglers, black Lucchesi's, and black belt with silver tip and buckle. They both looked appropriate for a western music show.

She turned when he was within ten feet, and her face changed from a pout to a broad smile. "I was beginning to wonder! Thought you got held up someplace."

"I make it a habit to be on time and not a minute early," he said, and they embraced with her giving him a peck on the cheek. "I'll get the tickets and we can go down the street for a drink." She followed him to the ticket booth. There were only two people ahead of him so it was quick.

He showed her the tickets and said, "We are in the balcony. I always liked that best here. Better view. Hope that's OK."

"Perfect! Let's get that drink. I'm dry as West Texas."

There was a little place just across the street and a half-block down, where they stood at the scarred, 100-year-old bar. She ordered a vodka Collins and he had a Beam and Coke with lots of ice. He said, "Do you want to eat dinner out or did you get something at the apartment?"

"I fixed a fruit plate and nice cheese tray for later. Hope that gives you enough strength for the workout I'm going to give you," and she laughed. "You got some kissing to do."

They drank quickly and fell into the line when the Aztec doors opened. The lobby of the Aztec was like something from a medieval dream mixed with Mexican heritage—beyond easy description. They took their time, looking at the huge Aztec calendar, the columns and walkways surrounding above the floor and the ridiculously large and ornate chandelier that hung above.

"This is the first time I have here in a couple of years. I had forgotten how amazing the place is. They don't make um like this anymore," she said as she looked up at the chandelier.

"Haven't been for a while. How many movie tickets at a quarter apiece do you think it would take to build a place like this back in 1926?"

"Too damn many!"

They ignored the concessions and climbed the staircase to the balcony and found their seats. Just like the tourists, they gazed at the dark, sky-blue ceiling with its twinkling stars, projected floating clouds, and the red-eyed Aztec idols on either side of the stage. The show actually started on time and they both laughed and sang along as the cast of local musicians and visiting artists did their thing. Darlene leaned against Doc's shoulder and occasionally put her hand on his leg. This was a woman for whom the sense of touch was important. Doc wondered if Jack Darling had the same affinity for the warm feel of her body or if he preferred the body of a bound Mexican whore.

When the show ended, they strolled down the River Walk among thousands of tourists and locals who crowded the concrete adjacent to the river diversion, where the tour boats and dinner cruises plied the little waterway. It was Friday and there were more people than the night before and, probably, less than there would be the next night. The walk was only fifteen minutes, and they climbed the stairs to the apartment's doorway. She punched in the numbers and they walked in.

"Fix me a vodka tonic with two lime slices, will you? And make yourself whatever you fancy. You know where everything is. I'm gonna freshen up a bit and get comfortable. Kick your boots off. We can eat a bite and talk. I want to know more about you." She took a fruit plate from the refrigerator and sat it on the bar next to a cheese assortment that had been left to ripen to room temperature. Then she waked to the bedroom and closed the door.

Doc found the ingredients and made her drink, strong, in a tall, frosted glass. He started on bourbon, so he decided to stay the course. No Jim Beam but he found a bottle of Blanton's, with the racehorse statuette on the cork.

He knew it was expensive—more expensive than what he normally drank, by a factor or five. He thought it was too special to adulterate with Coke, so he took it straight, over ice. Then he sat on one of the two barstools, nibbling a little wedge of Jarlsberg while he waited. He sipped the high-dollar whisky and nodded his approval.

Her return was worth the wait. She came back in the room bare-footed, wearing a pair of loose, white gym shorts and a white Longhorn football jersey, cut short, just long enough to cover her breasts. Number 11. She wore no bra and, he suspected, no panties. She sat in the other stool and leaned against its back, taking a long, double drink from her glass before setting it back down. She grabbed a handful of mixed nuts from the bowl and said, "OK, now I want to know everything there is to know about you. Don't leave anything out."

"Last night you said that kind of talk was boring. I'm sure, hearing about my life would put you to sleep."

"You may put me to sleep but it won't be with your story." She giggled, making Doc wonder if she had used the foil and straw while she was changing. Her eyes looked clear so he thought she hadn't. She took a long, very slim cigarette out of a pack on the bar and he lit it, as a gentleman should. She blew the smoke from the side of her mouth and said, "Well, I'm waiting."

He told her of his parents and his upbringing in small town America, his football experiences and injuries, his college days, early marriage. He stopped short at that point.

"Well, those are just life facts. There's more to the story than you are telling. Come on, big fellow. You can pour it out to me. Who am I going to tell?"

Doc thought for a moment. Some things are harder to tell than others. He decided to create the Reader's Digest Condensed version of his life—dropping from the doctoral program, divorce from his first wife, becoming a biker, falling in real adult love, and losing object of his affection. He summarized his professional life in a single, long, compound sentence. When he was done, he asked, "Is that enough or do you need more details. They are just as pedestrian as the quick tell."

"The biker thing and what you say about Kay—that could stand a lot more detail. I can tell that it made you uncomfortable to tell what you did so I won't ask for more. Not now, anyway."

They ate and made small talk for a while and each had a second drink and Doc was making a third when she said, "You know, I don't always act like I did last night. Well, maybe a little. I was a straight arrow until Jack. He's a kinky little bastard. He got us into some swinger sessions in Dallas and I found that pretty strange."

"Never done anything exactly like that. I mean, a little limited group sex kind of thing but never with a bunch of strangers. I probably couldn't get it up with a crane in something like that."

"Oh, Dallas was pretty nuts. There would be anywhere between 20 and 40 people at some of those parties. Fucking and sucking everywhere, with anybody. I mean there were only two kinds of men there. They are either macho bastards who think they are porn stars, or they are dumpy little men with tiny dicks who wish they were porn stars. And the women! Most of them are middle-aged housewives. Bored shitless and ready to screw anybody. It got old pretty quick. Austin was the same, after we moved there, but the parties were smaller and the people, a little more attractive."

Doc listened and said, "Well, I guess I'm just an old fuddy-duddy but that kind of thing holds no attraction for me. Just out of curiosity, is there a swinger scene in good old LaGrange?"

She was just taking a drink when he asked and she laughed out loud, until vodka tonic dripped from her nose. "Oh! Excuse me." She took a bar towel and wiped her face, still laughing. "LaGrange! Well, not so you'd know it. Oh, people get together. You know, maybe two couples who like one another. Something like that. But Jack is still kinky as hell. Sometimes—not often, but sometimes—he arranges for a younger woman. You know, one who likes men and women, to come play a little. I think that damn McDole may supply them, but Jack avoids telling me. They just show up and we have a little good, clean fun."

"Really! The state representative? Ain't that a kick in the head."

"I really think it may be that wife of his who has the connection. You know, she's Mexican. They call her Anna, but her real name is Liliana. Was Liliana Maria Perez before she married ol' Steve McDole. She's a bit younger than him—just had her forty-first birthday party. She was educated at SMU and has no accent anymore." She laughed and continued, "Unless she gets pissed off and then she can cuss up a blue streak in Spanish."

"I'll be damn! She seemed like such a prude when I met her at the SPJST dance."

"Oh, far from it! She thinks she's quite a hot tamale. We did a little switcheroo with them once but neither me nor Jack was impressed enough to get together again. But Jack stays close to McDole. He knows where the money is."

"I guess that's why Jack has started the shooting club. To be around money or for it to make him some extra cash?"

"Well, that's half right. Regardless of what Jack might say, he knows that place will never pay for itself. It's for him to make contacts. Jack has no skill at much of anything except being a popular guy. He makes friends easily and never forgets a face or name. Hell, he should have been the politician!"

"How about the little whip and the handcuffs. Is that you or Jack?"

"Damn! You gave me a good spanking last night. I liked it! No, Jack is a full-on S&M kind of guy, if left to his own devices. He loves bondage and that kind of stuff and I'm just not into the crazy shit. Handcuffs, dildos, a little spanking once in a while. Keeps the juices flowing for me. Let's go in the bedroom and get my juices flowing, Doc. All this talk is making me horny as hell."

Doc followed her into the bedroom where she stripped off the shorts and jersey and crawled under the sheet. "There's a joint in the drawer. Let's burn it and then get down to it. All natural tonight. No whips, no vibrators, no bells and whistles. Just the two of us. How would you like that?"

Doc shucked his boxers and flipped his socks into his boots. "I think that would be great for me but maybe I need some help in making you happy."

"No worries, sweetheart. You can handle the tough duty." And he did.

The next morning, Doc was, once again, the first to wake. He put on his shorts and jeans and padded into the kitchen and found the makings for coffee and brewed a pot in the Cuisinart. He was sitting at the bar sipping when she walked in, wrapped in a sheet.

"Babe, it's been great fun. Maybe we will do it again sometimes. I need to get back home today. Have a few things that need doing before Jack returns. I'm sure you can find something to do with yourself when I'm gone. You've about fucked me down, anyway," she said and smiled at him.

"I don't believe that last part for a minute. It was great. Let me know when you come back to town and maybe we can get together." She was by his side by then, picked up his coffee mug and took a long drink and washed it around in her mouth before swallowing.

"Believe what you want to believe," she said and gave him a good, coffee-tinged kiss. He dressed and they hugged and kissed again as she held the door open, still wrapped in her sheet. "*Adios,* darlin'," she said as he descended the stairs, holding his hand up to block the Texas sun from his eyes.

***

15.

On Sunday morning, Doc called Sal. "How are you doin' on this fine sabbath?" Doc asked when Sal got to the phone.

"Lucky you caught me. The reds are running now, and I was supposed to go catch some of them. Too windy today, so I slept in. Did you see sweet thing again?"

"Yeah, and I learned some things. I think maybe she and Jack are on the edges of the thing back in LaGrange. Maybe not directly involved but they know who is, I believe. You remember that Representative McDole? The one with the snooty wife?"

"Sure. Bastard couldn't shoot worth a shit. And his old lady had her nose up her own ass. What about them?"

"Seems the Darlings and McDoles are into some perverse shit. Bondage, Sado-masochism, that kind of stuff. And they are connected with the smack business, somehow. McDole and his ol' lady and Jack, anyway. Just haven't figured the angles yet. I don't think Darlene is involved except on the fun side. She's fun looking for a place to happen. Let's see if we can make a road trip back to LaGrange the next time you have Friday off."

"You keep thinking, Doc. That's what you're good at," and he laughed at his friend's expense. "Hell, I can get any Friday I want off. Just work an extra hour the other days. I'm trying to finish piping a chem process right now. How 'bout, maybe, the second Friday of November. Unless you are itching to go back before then. I could just meet you there or we could drop my van in Columbus and ride together in your Tahoe from there."

"Sounds good. I'll fill you in when we get together."

***

Doc worked and was his usual businesslike self for the next two weeks. His thoughts frequently went back to the nights he spent with Darlene Darling. He had been with many women in his life, but she was probably as beautiful and skillful as any he had known—possibly at the top of that list, but he never compared any woman to Kay. It wouldn't be justice for either the woman or his lost love. He knew the time with Darlene was simply a diversion for both of them and there was no emotional link created and neither of them had wanted one. Just a passing of two ships in the night, as they say. He doubted that the experience would ever be repeated but the memory would always be with him. He thought he was fortunate that, when exceptional things happened in his life, he was able to both appreciate them at the time and store them as wonderful memories. Not everyone was that lucky.

He also considered the relationship between the Darlings and the events in LaGrange. His feeling was that they were somehow connected but he hadn't quite figured out how deep the connection might be. One thing that kept flashing through his mind was the black and red car and the direction he was sure that it came from. Maybe it was a trick his memory was playing on him but, the more he thought about it, the more he was absolutely convinced that the car had come from the right side of the park. And driven away to the left, toward US Hwy 77.

That created a connection, along with the Darling home being to the right, combined with what Darlene had told him of Jack's fondness for group sex and S&M. It all seemed to indicate the possibility of their involvement—at least with the dead girl. Even though Darlene smoked a little skag from time to time, he found it difficult to believe she and Jack were behind the heroin distribution. He also considered what he had learned about McDole and his wife from Mexico. He had taken an immediate dislike for them both. That wasn't proof or evidence or anything more than a knee-jerk reaction of a man who considered himself a good judge of character. He tried to tell himself to just let the whole thing drop but then, in his mind's eye, he would see the girl, in her blue shift, disappear over the edge. He knew it would stay there—at least until there was some resolution.

These things played on Doc to the point that he had to talk to somebody and the only somebody he was willing to share with was Fat Sally Lombardo. So he called Sal on Monday night. It was Veteran's Day and he knew Sal refused to work on any holiday that he viewed as patriotic. When Lois answered and then put Sal on the line, Doc said, "Well, did you go fishing today?"

"Damn straight! Kicked ass on redfish and a few trout. Even caught a doormat flounder. What' up Doc?"

"Wish I could be there when Lois makes the grease stink. Hey, are we still on for Friday? I took a vacation day. We really need to talk. This whole thing is burning a hole in my head."

"You need to go fishing more often. Yeah, I did the same. Vacation, I mean, but the LaGrange thing is the farthest thing from my mind. Sure, I'll meet you in Columbus and we can go in your ride. I'll find a place to stash the van. Damn thing is covered with duct tape, so I don't think nobody is gonna want to steal it. Where and what time?"

"Let's get some lunch at Mikeska's and we can go on from there." And it was set.

On Friday, Sal arrived early and talked to the owner

of the barbeque joint, adjacent to I-10. The man agreed to let Sal park behind his business, so long as nobody could see the van from the highway. He figured it might scare people enough so they would drive on to the next restaurant down the highway.

When Doc walked in, Sal was drinking from a big plastic tumbler of iced tea. "I was about to order if you didn't show up pretty quick. I'm hungry as hell."

They ordered sliced brisket and sausage with a side of pinto beans and were sitting at a window table. Sal asked, "Why are you letting this shit eat you up? Can't you just turn it loose? Nothing we can do about any of it."

"Sal, I've been around three shootings in my life. The first time was back at Bob's shop in Sanctuary. The next two were in LaGrange. That's three times more than I ever figured on and I didn't like none of them. I think it just affected me, somehow. Getting to know Darlene Darling and hearing what she told me just added to it. Man, I just think I need some of what they call 'closure'."

"I guess I can see that. Hell, other than Nam, LaGrange was the only time I've been around it. I wasn't there when the thing went down at Bob's. I gotta tell you that I haven't lost a minute's sleep about taking out them two at the house. Had to be done. It was the only way and now there's two less assholes on the planet. Other than gooks, them are the only two I ever killed. I guess it's a good thing that I was the one who did it. I think it would have put you over the edge."

"I don't know. The only one I felt bad for was Hillman and that had nothing to do with that piece of shit brother-in-law of his getting what he had coming. Just felt bad for the man and his wife."

"Yeah, ol' Hillman probably hasn't got any leg since then. On the other hand, maybe mourning sex may be better than mornin' sex."

"You are incorrigible! I feel sorry for Lois. Well, eat up so we can get going. I brought my cellular telephone with me. Hope it works in LaGrange. I want to try to meet Darlene for a little talk."

"OK. You gonna eat that sausage? And hey, don't feel too bad for Lois. She's getting it twice a day whether she wants it or not."

"That's mighty big talk from a fifty-one-year-old fat man."

They drove up Hwy 71, talking all the way. Sal yearned for details about Doc's escapades with Darlene, so Doc obliged. That took up most of the half-hour trip. They pulled into the lot at the truck stop café. There was a sign out front saying that they were relocating to a new building out on the Hwy 71 bypass, which had just been completed. Doc took his phone from the console and punched in Darlene's number. She answered on the second ring. "Hello, who am I speaking to?" she wanted to know.

"This is Doc Quinn. I'm in LaGrange and thought I'd give you a call. Hope all is going well in your life."

"Well, what a surprise! It's all good. What are you doing in town?"

"Sheriff Hillman wanted a follow-up talk, so I just drove in," Doc lied. "Any chance of us having a drink or something?"

She thought for a long moment and then replied, "The drink will work but no chance for *or something*! I mean, that would be nice but Jack's in town. Why don't you meet me at that little beer joint where I first saw you? It's called Starters. You know, over on the east side of town."

"I know the place. Tell me when."

"Give me a half-hour. See you then." And she ended the call.

"OK, I'm gonna meet with her in thirty. What am I

gonna do with you. I think it might give her a case of lockjaw if you were with me."

"Well, thank you very fucking much. I bet I could find a game of 42 or moon if you drop me at the domino parlor close to the courthouse. Surely, some of them old men have learned English by now. I don't speak no Bohunk at all."

Doc dropped Sal at the domino parlor and drove to the beer joint. There was a shiny, new, black Mercedes SL600 parked close to the door. Only one other vehicle—an old Dodge pickup—was in the lot. It was only a little after one and working men were still working.

***

The bar was dark and Darlene was sitting at a corner table with a beer in front of her and another at the chair across the table. "Hello, Darlene. You look amazing. But what else is new?"

"Well, thank you for noticing. You look like . . . well . . . you. Which is just right. Did you meet with Sheriff Hillman yet?"

"Later today. Just killing time and I'd rather kill it with you than anybody else I can think of. Don't know if I told you or not but that was a lot of fun when I saw you in San Antone. Damn shame you don't live closer."

"You wouldn't want that. It would get in the way of your life, and I'd get boring for you after a while. That's just the way it works. It's better when it's a stolen treat. Don't you think?"

Doc thought a beat and said, "Probably right. We live in different worlds even if it's only a hundred miles apart."

"I know you didn't just want to kill time. What do you have on your mind? I mean, other than throwing me across this table and having your way with me," she laughed and he loved how she laughed.

"Nothing really. Just in town and hoped I could just visit with you. But I was thinking about something you told me back in San Antonio."

"What would that be?"

"Well—and I probably just shouldn't go there—I was thinking about what you said about having somebody coming in for a party sometimes. I mean, another woman. And I was thinking about the morning the girl jumped. I was wondering if she might have been one of the women who y'all partied with."

Darlene became sullen and he knew she was thinking behind her blue eyes. "Maybe I said too much. I was high and in a frisky mood. Frankly, I have no idea about that girl. I never saw her picture or anything. I guess it could have been, but I have no way of knowing. Let's talk about something else."

"You can't blame me for wondering. The car she ran from came from the direction of your house, I'm almost sure. Did you and Jack have company that night—the night before the girl jumped?"

"Oh, I really don't remember that night. It's been months ago. No reason to remember it." She lifted her purse from the back of her chair and started to stand. Doc gently put his hand on hers and she sat back down. "Look, I am not comfortable talking about what Jack and I do. Did. Whatever. I should probably just go now." She stood again and walked toward the door and Doc followed.

Outside, she clicked the lock button on her key fob and opened the door. Doc put his hand on the door. She gave him a forced 'come hither' look as she slowly swung her legs into the car, with her skirt sliding to mid-thigh and allowing him a look. She smiled and said, "It's been grand, Doc, but I don't think we need to see each other anymore. And you can't mention any of this to Hillman. There's nothing there. Do you understand?"

"I hear you darlin'. Sorry if upset you with anything I said. You enjoy your weekend."

She pulled her door shut, still smiling at him. "Be careful, Doc," she said, put the sports car in gear, revved the engine, and sprayed him with pea gravel as she sped from the lot.

Doc lit a cigarette and got back in his Tahoe. He sat there in the parking lot for a minute, trying to sort out what had just happened. He knew she was lying. He wondered if the San Antonio meeting had been designed to find out what he knew. Did she tell him what she wanted him to hear, back then? Didn't seem likely. Maybe she was really just high and it gave her the motor mouth when she should have stayed quiet? He thought it was time to talk to Sheriff Hillman but he had no idea what to say to the man.

He drove back downtown and saw Sal sitting on a bench in front of the domino parlor, talking to men who looked like old farmers. When Sal saw him, he shook hands with the men and Doc picked him up at the curb.

"Well, did you learn anything new?" Sal asked.

"Ol' Darlene knows something. I'm sure of it. She twisted off when I asked her about the night before the girl died. Let's go talk to Hillman. Damn DCI guy told me to go through Ryley but fuck um. I kinda like ol' Sheriff Hillman."

Doc parked in front of the Sheriff's Office, and they walked in to find Hillman leaning over Deputy Hlavinka's shoulder, studying some paperwork. Hlavinka smiled broadly when they walked in. Hillman didn't.

"What the hell are you old boys doing back in my county? Can't say I'm tickled to see you. I mean, seeing's how trouble follows y'all around like a puppy dog."

Doc spoke, "Just back in the area and were hoping to

catch up a little."

"Well, come on back to my office. Can't imagine we have much to discuss." As they were walking down the hall, he grumbled, "This is ballgame night. Leopards are gonna get their asses kicked by Sealy, but I have to be there. Head of the booster club, you know. Don't have much time for you two."

They walked in his office and took chairs by his desk. "OK, what is it you want to talk about?"

Doc said, "I've been thinking about all this. Hell, it's all I can think about sometimes. We just wanted to know if there's been any movement on the drug angle?"

Sal added, "Yeah, it kind of gets unnerving when people shoot at us. Any news you can share?"

"I ain't too happy about it and neither are the city cops here, but the DCI and Rangers have pretty much taken charge of the whole thing. I imagine the Feds are trying to bump the state guys out of their way. Word is the junkies are hurting in Dallas and Houston but that's always temporary. Somebody will fill the vacuum. The three women disappeared across the border along with the two shooters, but I expected that. No calls or visitors to the house—we're still keeping an eye on that."

"Yeah, a guy named Hankins tole me to contact Ryley if I wanted to know anything. Hankins said I met him here but I don't remember him. And I wasn't too impressed with Mr. Ryley. Like they say, I'd rather talk to the farmer—and you are the farmer as far as I'm concerned."

Hillman smiled and said, "Well, I appreciate that. Them guys have been making me feel like this is their problem. Hell, it's my problem. Not a day goes by that somebody don't ask what's happening with it all and I have to plead ignorance and I'm right. I'm out of the loop."

Doc said, "I have an unrelated question. What can you tell me about Jack Darling and Representative McDole?

I've been looking for a place to invest and I understand they have done well with their own money-making ventures. How's the sporting clays thing doing for Jack?"

"I don't know if I can tell you anything that will help you with that. Why don't you just go talk to Jack?"

"Does McDole represent Fayette County? I never got clear on that."

"No. His area is just north of Austin. Around Round Rock, but I'm not sure exactly which county he's representing. He does spend time around here. Has a place down on the Colorado south of here."

"How about his wife's family? I understand they are from Mexico and very rich. I wouldn't have never figured her for anything but a Texas girl."

"Yeah, everybody knows about that bunch. Her old man likes to catch bass in the lake here. Don't know if you have been there. Powerplant lake—called Fayette County Reservoir. I guess it's full of big bass. Wouldn't know, really, because I don't fish. Hunt but don't fish. He flies in on his own private plane. Keeps it at the strip out 71 northwest of town. Must be nice, being rich. I'll never know, not on a sheriff's pay."

"OK, I'll give Jack Darling a call and see if I can get some insight on how to get rich," said Doc.

"Look, I hate to cut this short, but I need to get over to the high school. Being head of the boosters is probably a bigger honor than being sheriff. We're talking Texas high school football, after all," said Hillman, and he sounded like he believed it.

***

"What do you say we take a little drive up to Monument Hill? Not the park but I'd like to take a look at where Darling lives," Doc said, when he and Sal were back in his Tahoe.

"Might as well. Can't dance. Let's do it."

The drove back down the main drag and turned right on US 77, then across the bridge and up the twisting road to the top of the bluff. They turned right again on the road that ran past the Monument Hill park. The parking lot was empty, except for one pickup and an old sedan. They thought those must belong to the old lady behind the information desk and one or other of the park rangers they had met. They continued down the road and slowed for the very sharp left curve and into the residential area.

"Do you have a street name or anything for Darling?" Sal asked.

"Nope. It can't be so big up here that we couldn't find it. At least, if his Corvette or her Mercedes is in sight."

It proved easier than that. The houses all had street-side mail boxes. They drove down the short, curved streets and at the end of the second one was a brick-mounted box. It announced 'Darling' in carefully lettered gold leaf on the black metal box. The house was impressive—the ranger had told them on the last trip that it was the biggest one on the hill. Gray brick, two-story with dormer windows and a wide, cut-glass front door. As they slowed at the double drive, the right-side door of the triple garage started to open, so Doc stopped. The maroon Vette's engine raced, and the car jumped back toward Doc's Tahoe, and then slammed to a stop. Jack Darling got out, smiling the same smile he always had. He walked out to Tahoe and Doc punched down his window.

"Well! What in the world are y'all doing back in LaGrange? After the mess this summer, I'm surprised to see you around here again."

"We had to talk to Sheriff Hillman. I am just using the excuse to look at some property. Kind of planning my retirement and this might be just the kind of place I'd like," said Doc.

Darling leaned against the side of Doc's ride and nodded at Sal. "You know, property values in Fayette County are pretty manageable but it gets kind of pricy here on the hill."

"I may not be in your tax bracket, but I do OK," said Doc, with a chuckle. Just then he saw the front door of the house open and Darlene step out. When she saw Doc, she stopped, started to step back and push the door shut but then decided to come out. She wasn't smiling. She walked toward them.

Jack said, "We were just going to get a bite to eat and then go to the ballgame. I bet Hillman mentioned it when you met with him. He's the team's biggest fan. He was a star end there when he was in school."

Sal spoke, as Darlene joined her husband. "I was kinda hoping that y'all might be busting some clays tomorrow. We were probably hanging around tonight. Getting late for driving back to Deer Park. Maybe we'll go to the game."

Darling, still smiling, said, "Don't have any group coming down this weekend. Why don't I call my man, Sam, and set something up. Might invite some of the guys I see at the game. Hey, why don't you just stay out there tonight. I can get Sam to make sure two of the rooms are presentable and wait around there for y'all. Save you the price of a hotel." Behind her husband, Darlene lifted her sunglasses and her eyes said she wasn't pleased.

Doc ignored her stare. "Jack, that's too much! But we would really appreciate your hospitality. You sure it won't be too much trouble?"

"Not at all. I'll have Sam's wife come out and cook in the morning. Darlene and I will join you for breakfast. How's that sound?"

"That would be great! We really appreciate it. Can

we just grab some dinner here in town and then head out there for the night?"

"I'll run back inside and call Sam." And the Darlings walked back to the house as Doc and Sal drove away.

"What the fuck? Ol' Darlene was drilling holes in you with her eyes. She's probably giving Jack what for right now for extending the invite," said Sal.

"It should be interesting. Let's hit the guy with the drag-behind barbeque pit and pick up some supper and take it to the big barn."

***

16.

After hitting the rolling barbeque man, they tossed their package of meat and white bread into Doc's Cooler. Then they stopped and picked up a 6-pack of Lone Star and fresh Ice. Doc said, "Before we head to the shooting club, let's drive down toward the smack house. There's something I want to see."

"Damn, Doc! Can't you let this shit drop for five minutes? Have a beer and kick back. I'd even be OK with you smoking a damn cigarette. Whatever."

"I just want to see something." He drove by the Fayette airport and checked his odometer from there to the turnoff to the house. "Less than four miles. That'd be pretty convenient for somebody from Mexico with a private plane. Don't you think?"

"What I think is that you are trying to play detective and it's driving us both nuts."

"What the hell else would we be doing on a November weekend? Too windy on Galveston Bay to fish. You said so, yourself. And we'll get to do some shooting tomorrow. You like to shoot. So just shut the fuck up and let me do whatever it is that I'm doing. Whatever the hell that is."

"Tell me some more about ol' Darlene. Damn, I'd like a shot at that!"

It was a retelling, but Doc complied and they arrived at the big barn when the sun was about to set. The big Mexican named Sam was standing by the sliding doorway. It was just opened about four feet, to allow the outside air flow through.

When they parked and got out, Sam walked toward

them. "Mr. Jack said y'all was comin'. Got rooms for you fixed up. You can put your truck inside if you want to. Sposed to rain tonight, maybe."

Doc said, "That won't be necessary. It could use a washing, anyway." And they followed Sam into the expanse of the big building.

"My wife be here to cook for you guys and Mr. and Mrs. Darling early tomorrow." He showed them to rooms 3 and 4 on the far end of bottom level. "Got satellite TV and you can use the AC or open the windows and use the ceiling fans. Gonna get down in the 50s tonight. There's beer and stuff at the bar and in the ice box. I'll be going. Got a family thing tonight. Y'all be OK?"

Sal said, "We'll be fine. You go and enjoy your family. Thanks." And Sam walked back out, got in his pickup, and drove away, leaving Doc and Sal alone in the barn. They picked their rooms and brought in their duffel bags—both had packed some extra clothes, assuming they'd be away from home overnight. Sal hadn't got his pistol back from Sheriff Hillman yet and it concerned him. He seldom left home without some kind of gun, so he had his 9MM Browning Hi-Power in his bag. He took it out and put it in the drawer of his bedside stand. Doc had brought his own Glock 17 but it was locked in the console of his Tahoe. He didn't expect to need it but better safe than sorry.

After checking their rooms, they walked over to the kitchen area. Sal was carrying the package of smoked brisket, sausage, and bread. "There's a microwave. I'll heat up supper. Find us a fancy beer in the fridge."

There were several *fancy* brands of beer in the refrigerator. "You want a European beer of a Mexican beer."

"I ain't particular, long as it ain't light beer. Don't want none of that goat piss. Got any Dos Eques? I like the brown bottle."

"Got um!" said Doc and they sat at one of the folding tables with its folding chairs and made quick work of the brisket and sausage. Just as before, it was excellent and proper for men in Texas—barbeque for lunch and barbeque for dinner. They never even questioned the need for a vegetable.

"What kind of shit are you planning for tomorrow? I mean, with Jack? I know you got something on your mind," said Sal.

"Hell, I don't know. I'll just play it by ear. I don't mind giving up Darlene. I mean, letting Jack know that I probably know more than I should. Let's just see who shows up for breakfast."

"I gotta admit that there are way too many coincidences around here. Don't know if Hillman gives a shit about any of it. He sounded like it was all with the state guys now. I think he has just about washed his hands of the whole damn mess."

Doc got up and pulled two more beers from the fridge and sat back down. "Maybe it's just me, but nobody else seems to think there's any kind of connection with Darling or McDole or Anna McDole's old man. And the location of the house so close to the airport and Perez coming and going in his private airplane. Maybe somebody should connect the dots for the cops. I'm not sure which cops—but some kind of cops."

"I think it's mostly in your mind, Doc. Maybe nobody sees any connection because there ain't no connection. Besides, McDole and some rich Mexican may have something like diplomatic immunity. Not really but, well, really. Wonder if *Señor* Perez is any kind of bureaucrat or something—or maybe an elected official—back across the border. Did Darlene mention anything about that?"

"No, she only said he was really rich and that Anna

had gone to school in Texas and didn't have any accent until she got to cussing and then it was pure border town. As corrupt as Mexico is, given that he has money, I'm sure he has some political pull down there."

They finished their beers and retired to their rooms. They had satellite TV, and both laid in their beds and channel surfed until they got sleepy. They opened their windows and turned the ceiling fans on and enjoyed the cool autumn air as it circulated through the big barn.

***

Doc was awakened by noise out on the open floor of the barn. He got up and looked out his window. He saw the same Mexican woman who had cooked for them when they had shot clays before. He turned back into the room, wondering if he should make the bed or strip it for washing. He decided to just half make it up—straightening the sheets and fluffing the pillows would have to do. Then he washed up a bit and brushed his teeth and put on yesterday's jeans and a long-sleeve fishing shirt. When he walked out his door he looked to his left and saw Fat Sally standing in his own doorway, wearing only his jockey shorts and yawning as he surveyed the building.

"Damn man! Put on some clothes. There's a lady out there."

"You know the value I put on clothes. I just use them to cover my naked ass, when absolutely necessary. Besides, my belly hangs down far enough there wouldn't be nothing to see if I didn't have no drawers on."

"Get dressed!" said Doc and he walked across the floor to the kitchen area.

"Hola señora. Buenos días," Doc said in his best

southern accented Spanish.

The woman replied, "Oh, you speak Spanish?"

"Not really. Just faking it. Didn't know if you spoke English," said Doc.

"Can't live around here your whole life without speaking English. I even speak a little Czech and a little German. Used to come in handy with some of the old folks. I worked as a maid at the old hospital. My name's Lupe."

"Great! We can understand one another. But don't drop any Czech or German on me," Doc said, and they both laughed. Sal was now dressed and walking toward them. He had overheard Doc and Lupe.

"*Hola, Lupe!* Got any coffee cooked yet?" Sal asked.

"It's brewed," she said and pointed to the line of coffee makers sitting on a table against the wall. There were Styrofoam cups, sugar and creamer. The men both got a cup and sat at the table, watching the woman go about her duties.

"Do you work for the Darlings all the time or just when he has people out here?" Doc asked Lupe.

"I clean house for Mrs. Darlene twice a week and for Mr. and Mrs. McDole when they are staying at their place down on the river. Mr. Jack, he's really good to me and Sam. Pays us full time. Sam does some things for Mr. Jack. Here and other places."

"That's awful nice of Jack. What kind of things does Sam do for him?" Sal said.

Just then Sam walked through the rear sliding door. He was wearing a rain hat and slicker. "Started to rain 'round midnight. It's a little sloppy out there but I think the rain is about done. Should be dried out enough to shoot some by the time y'all eat breakfast. I'll load the launchers when the rain quits altogether." He had the same severe face as always and Doc wondered if the man ever smiled.

Sal said, "We was just talkin' about you. Wondering

what kind of work you do for Jack. Your missus here says y'all work for him full time. Didn't know he had any kind of business around here."

"He don't. Not really. I take care of this place and do whatever else Mr. Jack asks me to do. You know, cutting limbs and keeping his place on the hill all pretty. Making sure he has firewood for his fireplace and smoker, and for the fire pit here. I'm a pretty good handyman too."

"Do you know when the Darlings will be out here? He said he might invite some other folks to shoot," said Doc.

"Don't know nothing about that. He called me early and just said to make sure y'all was taken care of. It ain't eight yet. I figure he'll be here before nine."

Lupi asked, "Do you want to eat now or wait for the others?"

Doc and Sal looked at each other and Sal said, "We can just wait 'till they all get here. Otherwise, we might have to eat breakfast twice." Lupe laughed. Sam didn't. He removed his hat and slicker and hung them over a chair. He got a cup of coffee and sat opposite of Doc and Sal.

"Why you men comin' back around here again? Thought y'all went home after the shit that went down in LaGrange last summer," Sam asked.

Doc said, "Had to talk to the Sheriff again. Also might be interested in getting some land around here. I need to think about getting me a place to retire someday. I kind of like this area."

"Ain't no place for you to live. It's just a lazy town. Nothin' goin' on round here. And the land prices are going through the roof. Man like you needs a place on a lake or down on the Gulf."

"Representative McDole has a place on the river south of here. He must think it's a nice place to settle down. I'm just looking. Always trying to find a place to put some money. You know, an investment. With land prices on the rise, maybe this is a good place to invest in land now."

"Well, you do what you want. Your money," said Sam.

Sal said, "What can y'all tell us about McDole and his father-in-law, *Señor Perez*?"

Lupe jerked around and looked at Sal and then her husband. Then she turned back to her kitchen duties.

Sam put his cup down on the table—hard—splashing some coffee on Formica. "I can't tell you nothin' 'bout nothin'." He got up, put his slicker and hat back on and walked out the back door.

Sal didn't turn it loose. "Lupe, you work at the McDoles' place. Is there anything you can tell us? I mean, Mr. McDole seems to have plenty of connections with people with money and power. We'd like to be able to make some of them connections too." Lupe didn't answer. She just kept scrubbing a pan that was already clean.

Doc said, "Sorry, Lupe. We don't want to step on anybody's toes. Just trying to learn the ropes around here."

She put the pan and SOS pad down, dried her hands and walked to the table where Doc and Sal were sitting. "Sam was right. We don't know nothin'. Maybe some folks should be left alone. You need to ask them kind of questions to Mr. Jack." She started to walk back to the sink.

"Does Perez stay with McDole when he comes into town to fish?" Sal asked.

Lupe stopped and thought for a moment, then turned back to them and said, "Can't hurt, I guess. Sometime he stays there—McDole's place—and, sometime he stay here. He always got two men traveling with him. I guess his pilot stays in town or someplace. That's all I'm gonna say 'bout any of these folks. They treat us good and I just ain't sayin' nothin' more. OK?"

Doc and Sal finished their coffee and got refills. They

walked toward the front door of the building and Doc lit a cigarette and they leaned against the sliding door, staying clear of the light rain, which was still falling. Sal looked at the sky and said, "Looks like it's gonna clear up. See blue sky's showing to the northwest."

"What do you make of Sam's attitude? And Lupe's? He's just not friendly. Don't seem to like us much. She seems like a sweet lady, though," said Doc.

"I think they are afraid you might get in their pocketbook. They have a pretty good gig going with Darling. Don't want you fuckin' it up."

***

As they stood in the gap in the big sliding door, Jack Darling's Corvette turned into the driveway, followed by a black Lincoln. Steve McDole was driving the Lincoln. Darling got out, closed his car door, and hustled through the rain to the doorway. Smiling as always.

"Hope you fellas had a good night. Darn Leopards got their asses kicked pretty good. I couldn't find anybody wanting to shoot today. Well, except Steve. Called him and he was willing."

Doc spoke, "We had a great night. Thanks for the hospitality. Quite a place you have here. We were expecting Darlene and some other folks to make it a contest today."

"She'll be right along. You know women. Always keep men waiting." By then, McDole had wrapped a plastic raincoat around himself and was dodging puddles on his way to the door. Everyone shook hands and they walked to the table by the kitchen area.

"Lupe! What kind of treat do you have for us this morning?" asked Darling.

"I'm making some buttermilk biscuits with cream gravy and whatever kind of eggs y'all want. 'Bout to put the biscuits in the oven now. That be OK, Mr. Jack?"

"That's just right! Be sure to put more black pepper in the gravy. I like it spicy," Darling said to the woman and turned to Doc and Sal and continued, "Lupe is one hell of a cook. Her biscuits are as good as I ever ate." McDole smiled and nodded his approval.

Sam had heard the cars pull up and he walked back in the rear door, in his slicker and hat. He walked up to his wife and they spoke low and in Spanish. Her face turned from a smile to a frown as he talked to her. Then he removed the rainwear and hung them on a rack by the row of rooms and stood, looking at the men at the table.

They all heard another vehicle crunching across the gravel. Sam walked to the front door and called back to the men, "Miss Darlene and Mrs. McDole got here. I'll take them an umbrella." And he pulled one from a bin near the front door and scurried out to help the women. The rain had all but stopped but he held the umbrella over their heads as they walked from Darlene's Mercedes and into the building.

The women crossed the concrete floor toward the table. They both forced smiles as they took their seats. Doc could tell that Darlene's eyes weren't smiling. She said to Anna McDole, "You remember these fellows from this past summer. Doc—Connor Quinn—and this fellow is Sal. Sorry, I have forgotten your last name," she said to Sal. Anna McDole did not smile and looked at Sal like he was something she needed to scrape from her shoe.

"Salvatore Lombardo. So happy to see you again, ladies." He thought he might just have to let Anna know just how obnoxious he could be. He'd been around wealthy people throughout his early life and hated their smug countenance. Both women just nodded.

Lupe brought cups of coffee to the women, along with a sugar bowl and cream pitcher. They nodded their acknowledgement and added powder and paint to their cups. "Breakfast be ready in a minute. Everyone want fried eggs?" Everyone did except for Anna McDole. Lupe fried the eggs and put them on individual plastic plates. She had laid out tableware and set up the biscuits and gravy, butter, strawberry jam, fig preserves and a jar of honey. Everyone took their plates and served themselves what they wanted and sat back down. Anna just buttered a biscuit and scooped the figs onto her plate. When everyone else had fixed their plates, Sam and Lupe made their own from whatever was left and sat at the table farthest from where the others were.

Jack Darling said to the group, "I think the rain has stopped. By the time we are done eating, I think it will be dried up enough to go bust some clays." He was smiling, as always. They made small talk through breakfast. Needed the rain, farmers had a good harvest, football team was not good, and the like. As they talked, Sam finished his food quickly and went into the gun room and took a case of clays outside to load the launchers.

"Are we all going to shoot today?" Darling asked and everyone indicated they would, except Anna McDole, who just shook her head. The shooters walked into the gun room and picked out their weapon of choice. Darlene chose a 20 gauge this time—a side-by-side—and everyone else picked 12-gauge guns of various types. Sam was at his station with the remote control for the clay throwers. It was decided that everyone would just shoot from ground-level this time. The wooden towers were slick from the rain.

Darlene shot 20 shells first, two at a time, hitting all 20 clays. Everyone clapped but nobody was surprised. Sal was next and he hit 18. When he finished, he walked over to Anna McDole, who shuffled a step farther away as he picked his place to stand. Darling was next on the shooter's pad. Sal said, "I understand you are from Mexico. I'd have never thought that. I mean you don't speak with an accent and you are very fair complected. I heard your father was a big man south of the border."

She just looked at the side of Sal's face, took a step farther away, and said, "My father is a respected man in Mexico and in America. And, what? Do you think that all Mexicans are brown like Indians or laborers? You do us an injustice, sir!"

"Oh, so sorry. Didn't mean to talk bad about Mexican people. I love Mexico and the people there. Well, except them that's got Juarez and the other border towns fucked up with the drug shit." He leaned toward her and again said, "Sorry." And, as he walked away managed a low velocity fart that he was sure the woman could hear but nobody else could. She covered her face with her hand and walked back to the building's back door. Her husband noticed and took on a quizzical expression.

The shooting continued until everyone had gone through the rotation twice. Doc and McDole were bad. Sal was good but not great. Darlene continued perfect and Jack was average. Afterward, Sam collected the shotguns and everyone went back into the building. "How about an Irish coffee? I feel like one. Who would like to join me?" Darling offered. Everyone agreed and they sat, while Lupe brewed a fresh pot. Darling opened a cabinet against the wall and moved bottles around until he found a bottle of Teeling, which he brought to the table. When the coffee had made, Lupe brought everyone mugs and spoons—no Styrofoam this time, but heavy stoneware mugs. She also took a can of Reddi Whip from the refrigerator.

"I'll show you how to do this," said Jack. "One of the great pleasures from the old sod." He poured a strong shot of the whisky into his coffee, dumped in two spoons of sugar and stirred it well. Then he topped it with a glob of the whipped cream. The others followed suit, making the drink to their own tastes. Sal opted for no whipped cream.

"Mind if I smoke while we have our coffee?" asked Doc.

Darlene responded, "No problem as long as you can give me one." Doc reached across the table, and she pulled a Marlboro from his pack and he held his butane lighter for her. She took a drag and blew the smoke directly in Doc's face. No one seemed to notice. Doc lit his own and sat back down. Lupe—always attentive—brought two metal ashtrays and sat them on the table.

Anna took one from a pack of Parliaments in her purse and Steve lit it for her. He didn't smoke. His face had become serious, for no apparent reason and he virtually hid behind his coffee mug.

Doc said, "Steve, I understand you have a place down on the river. I am interested in investing in some land and I kind of like it around here."

McDole's expression hardened further, and he said, "Mr. Quinn, I have become a pretty good reader of people. Last night at the ballgame, I spoke to Sheriff Hillman, and he told me that you paid him a surprise visit yesterday. Said he hadn't asked you two to come in to talk about the unfortunate events of this summer, or anything else. You just showed up. Is that true?"

"We thought there might be some things we could learn about that whole mess. It was something I hadn't experienced before and it kind of sticks in my craw. Do you know anything about it? He said the state boys have taken over the investigation. You being in state government, I thought you might have some insight," said Doc.

"Why don't you tell us what you really have on your mind."

"OK. It may be nothing but there's more here than meets the eye. I'm just interested in learning what that might be."

Jack Darling said, "OK folks, If we are going to talk serious business here, I think the ladies may want to head back to town." He looked at Sam, who was still sitting at the far table with Lupe. They stood up and Sam handed his truck keys to his wife, and she walked to the door.

"Well, I'm not going anywhere! I want to hear this," said Darlene. Her husband looked at her and his eyes tightened but he didn't say anything more.

McDole turned to his wife and said, "Why don't you take the Lincoln back home. Jack will give me a ride. Keys are in the car." She looked around in confusion before getting up and walking out the front door. They heard Sam's old pickup and the Lincoln start and drive toward the road.

"OK, it's just us guys now," said Sal as he glanced at Darlene. "Let's fucking talk."

McDole said, "OK Quinn, you have the floor. What's on your mind?"

Doc thought about how to respond. He had played this in his head before but felt he was ill prepared. He wanted to ask the right questions in the right order. Looking at McDole, he said, "Well, if I am going to live around here, I need to know where to find a little companionship from time to time. I'm older but I'm not old and I still have some needs. I understand you might know where a man could locate that kind of female companionship."

Darling was furious and stood and slammed his fist on the table. He glared at his wife then looked at Doc. "Steve, I think I know where he got that shit." And then he looked back at Darlene and growled, "What the fuck did you tell this son-of-a-bitch when you had *dinner* with him? Goddamnit!"

"Oh, Jack! Settle down, will you? This is no big deal.

He's just fishing," said Darlene. She was angry but didn't know if her anger was stronger for Jack or Doc.

McDole looked at Doc and said, "You still haven't told me what's on your mind. It isn't *companionship*!"

Sal was sitting quietly, taking it all in, and wishing he had his little Browning in his pocket.

"Alright. What I really want to know is if that girl who went off the cliff had spent the night with Jack and Darlene. Or with them and you and Anna. What can you tell me about that? She died for no reason, and somebody caused it. I am not going to rest until I know what happened."

Jack spoke up, "Why in the hell would you think she was at my house?"

"That's the way it stacks up. The car she was in came from your direction. She had been bound—possibly with handcuffs. And her feet had been tied up. You and Darlene like to play games with girls. You, Steve, supply girls. Both of you are perverted in your sexual habits. Darlene uses that Mexican brown smack to heighten her good times. Anna's father is a Mexican big shot, but nobody will say how he gets his money. The airport where he lands his plane is close to the house where the heroin was being cut and bagged. Why the damn law hasn't connected these dots is beyond me."

McDole, Darling and even Sam were transfixed by what Doc said. Darlene shook her head and looked at her feet. Sal just watched. Alert.

Finally, McDole said, "Sir, you are delusional."

Darlene spoke up, "Delusional or not, this shit isn't something the law needs to hear." Looking at Doc she growled, "Did you tell Hillman any of this?"

"Nope. It's just between us kids. I didn't know if there was any fire under this smoke—until now."

Everyone was quiet for a long beat and then Jack

Darling said, "Steve, why don't you take my Vette and go on home. Let me and Darlene deal with this. You need plausible deniability."

McDole didn't speak but stood up and Jack tossed him his keys and he headed for the front door. They all heard the Vette roar and disappear out to the pavement, where its tires squealed as he sped away.

"I had more questions I wanted to ask but I guess you can answer them," Doc said to Darling.

Darlene was sitting next to her husband and her purse was between them. He reached down and pulled a tiny .380 from the purse and aimed it at Doc's forehead. "I don't think we want to answer any more questions. But maybe I'll tell you some things to sort this out." He looked at the pistol in his hand and continued, "I want this to end peacefully. This is just for in case it doesn't," he said, waving the gun.

Sal said, "Ease up there, Bubba! We are all friends here. Let's just talk. You can probably find a way to make us go away. I mean, without us going away permanently."

"What do you have in mind, fat man?"

"Look man, you have money. McDole has money. Shit, even Doc has money. I don't have money. Doc and me ain't exactly as close as you might be led to believe. You getting my drift?" Doc was looking at his friend, confusion painted on his face.

To his wife, Darling said, "Go over to the gun room and get me a real pistol." Then he looked at Sam, who had been staring at everything that was happening. "Sam, get you a shotgun, too."

Darlene and Sam walked toward the gun room, which was on the back side of the building, next to the guest room, where Sal had slept. Darlene walked backward, keeping an eye on the table and the three men sitting there.

"How do you think you are getting out of this shit?"

said Doc. "The best thing you can do is just settle down and let's all go talk to Hillman. You're just a guy who likes to have a little fun. Everybody loves you. It's not too late."

"Shut the fuck up! Let me think," said Jack. By then Darlen and Sam were walking out of the gun room, armed to the teeth. Sal saw a chance and, in one huge move, lifted the table and toppled it over on Jack Darling. Doc jumped and ran toward the front door, thinking he could retrieve the Glock from his Tahoe, forgetting that he didn't even have the key, which was on his night stand.

Darlene was carrying a stainless Smith and Wesson .357 magnum. She aimed it at the ceiling over Doc's head and fired. The roar subsided just enough for him to hear her scream, "Stop, motherfucker!" And Doc did, raising his hands and turning to see her pointing the revolver from him to Sal and back again.

Sal had fallen back, tripping over his own chair when he flipped the table. He was still trying to untangle himself and get to his feet. Jack Darling was pushing the table away and trying to regain his faculties. He was bleeding from a cut across his forehead, where the table had smashed into him. He had dropped his pistol but found it on the concrete. He picked it up and raised it, aiming at Sal. Sam had dropped his shotgun, exited the rear door and was running along the tree line behind the building. He wanted no part of what was happening.

The standoff lasted only a few seconds but, to all of them, it seemed much longer. Then Darlene walked behind Doc and poked him in the back with her pistol. "Go sit down, asshole!" she said and the two of them walked slowly back toward the table, which Jack had pushed upright when he stood. When Doc and Darlene were still fifteen feet away, Sal, who was standing, turned and rushed toward the room where his pistol still rested in the bedside drawer. Jack shot once but missed as the big man disappeared through his door. Darlene tried to make herself shoot Doc, but she couldn't do it. She smacked him on the side of his head with the heavy barrel of the gun and Doc went to his knees.

She looked at Jack and said, "What now?" She was panicking and Jack wasn't any better. Neither of them had killed before and the first time is the hardest.

"I don't know! We can't let them go. We're fucked," said Jack, with terror in his eyes.

Sal cracked the door, pistol in hand, and saw Doc on his knees, holding his head. He exploded out of the door and shot once but missed Jack. Darlene was standing directly between Sal and her husband. She turned to her left and, as she did, Jack fired. He was a terrible shot with the tiny .380 but the bullet found its mark. Just not where he intended. It struck his wife's perfect right cheek bone, just below her eye. She was dead before the gun fell from her hand.

Jack Darling froze and, in a calm voice, said, "Oh shit." He dropped his gun and just stared at his wife lying on the concrete floor. Sal had a dead aim but didn't fire. He just ran to his friend's side.

"Brother! Are you OK?"

"What the fuck happened?" Doc mumbled, rubbing the side of his head.

"I think it's over. Just stay here 'till your head's better. It'll be OK." He looked at Jack Darling, who was still standing immobile, staring at his wife's lifeless body.

"You had me worried when you were trying to make a deal with them. It was bullshit. Wasn't it?" said Doc.

"What the fuck do you think?"

***

"Oh, my God!" was all that Sheriff Hillman could say

when he walked into the big metal building. Two deputies had arrived before the Sheriff. One was Johnny Lopez. He had bagged the .357 taken from beside Darlene's dead hand, and Sal's Browning and the little .380. Doc was sitting, holding a sandwich bag filled with ice, and wrapped in a dishtowel to his head, which Johnny had made for him. His head was hurting like hell. Jack Darling was handcuffed in the back of Lopez's squad car with his mouth open, his mind a blur. Sal was drinking a beer and leaning against the kitchen sink.

Hillman spoke to Lopez and the other deputy for several minutes. Then he motioned Sal over to the table where Doc was sitting. Sal grabbed another Dos Equis from the fridge before sitting.

"What is the hell happened here? You two are in deep shit! Goddamnit! I knew there would be hell to pay when you dropped by the office yesterday."

"Hey Sheriff! Don't be so hasty here. We didn't shoot anybody. Fuckin' Jack Darling shot his wife trying to take me out." He pointed to the roof, at a tiny hole thirty feet above. "And the bitch shot that hole in the roof." Then he pointed at a hole in the metal siding, just above the kitchen sink. "I shot that hole in the wall, trying to keep them Darlings from killing us. Check my pistol." Then, as an afterthought, "Dammit! I guess you're gonna want to keep my Browning. If you do that, just gimme back my 1911. Unless you took a liking to it for your own collection."

"Son-of-a-bitch! I knew you two were trouble. Yeah, I'll give your goddamn .45 back but we will probably need the 9, at least until ballistics has a chance to look at everything. Hell of a way to waste my fucking Saturday afternoon. The Aggies are on TV. Shit!"

***

Doc and Sal spent the night at the Riverview. Seemed like the logical place to them. On the way, Doc got checked out at the ER at the hospital. The doctor told him he was lucky to have a hard head. When Sal heard him say that, he laughed and said, "Doctor, you got no idea!"

After church on Sunday, they were all back at the Sheriff's office conference room. Same cast of characters as in last summer and nobody was happy. There wasn't much conversation and the officials just glanced at one another—uncomfortably. Naiser was running the meeting. They were missing the Cowboys game and that added to their ire. The Ranger, Ryley, Hankins, and the others were all there. DA Madilyn Bartos was in the meeting and very interested—she was evidently not a football fan. Doc noticed the Ryley seemed distracted. Doc and Sal both had to tell their stories, separated from one another. When they came back together, Bartos said, "There's nothing we can hold you on but I'm sure we will have to get you two back here for some hearings and the like."

This perked up Hillman, who said, "Oh, shit! Do we really need them to come back again?" and he just shook his head.

Doc spoke, "I am obviously not a police officer. Never have been. But I think there are some things you need to look into."

John Naiser said, "Are you trying to do our job for us? Or are you just getting in the way?"

"No sir. I just think this is more complicated than anybody may have considered. I mean, several departments have been looking at this and I don't know who's really running this show or how much you really communicate with one another."

Naiser rolled his eyes and said, "OK, what do you think we are missing that you are able to see, Mr. oilfield supply man?"

Sal laughed and said, "You might want to listen, Major."

Doc said, "First, I think Jack Darling can tell you everything you need to put the hurt on some important people. He'd give up his mama if he thought it would keep him out of serious shit. He's a fucking coward who's been riding on other peoples' coattails all his life."

Hillman said, "Just what do you think he can tell us?"

"I don't believe he is involved with anything heavy. I mean, he's no heroin smuggler. He's no killer. Well, unless you consider him accidently killing his wife. He has some unusual sexual habits. They pretty much admitted that the girl who jumped off the cliff had spent that night at his house. His wife liked to smoke skag. I think he has serious dirt on the Honorable Mr. Steve McDole, who I believe is a crook. Not that it would eliminate him from public office in Texas." Several in the room snickered at that. "I think this would all lead you to Anna McDole's father. He's a bigwig in Mexico and I think he's the one behind the heroin thing."

Ryley spoke up, "And I believe you are full of shit. This is ridiculous."

"Maybe I am. I don't have any evidence, but you folks are all in the business of taking down bad guys. Ol' Jack Darling can help you do that if you lean on him just a little bit."

Naiser said, "This is all very interesting, and we will take it under advisement. Until then, I suggest you get the hell out of town. I know the Sheriff wishes you would stay away but that's up to you, at least until Ms. Bartos needs you back here."

Hillman said, "If nobody has anything else, can we all get home in time for our Sunday dinner." Nobody spoke against it so the meeting broke up. Doc and Sal followed the Sheriff down to his office where he handed Sal his model 1911. No bullets. And then he ushered them out of the building. On the front steps, he said, "I know I've been kind of hard on you boys but I gotta give it to you. This whole thing might have gone unsolved. Things just fade away with passing time. Y'all have stirred it up to the point that I believe something will get done." He paused a beat, smiled, and said, "You know, you were right about another thing. Too damn many chiefs and not enough Indians bumping into one another. But I never said that."

They turned away, toward Doc's Tahoe and Hillman called to them, "But don't let me catch your sorry asses back in Fayette County again. You got it!" He said it with a smile. They waved back at him and were out of town, down 71, within ten minutes.

Jack Darling spilled everything he knew in the matter and about everyone involved. He copped a plea for voluntary manslaughter in the death of his wife and served 23 months in a minimal security country club state prison. Later he and his smile returned to Austin but most of the old doors were closed to him. Hillman didn't run for Sheriff again when his term was up. He had enjoyed all he could stand. He bought the gun club building from the Darling estate and turned it back into a construction company, with the help of friends and relatives. He prospered. Representative McDole resigned from the legislature after his wife left him and he moved to Florida. *Señor* Perez didn't enter the United States for several years and he was greeted at the Miami airport by DEA officers when he did. Ryley disappeared and his whereabouts are unknown, even to his family. And Johnny Lopez joined the Texas State

Highway Patrol.

***

Epilogue

December can be a great time to fish the Galveston Bay system. Or it can suck. On the 8th of that December it was just right. Morning lows in the 50s, warming to around 70 by midday. Just a 5mph breeze from the southeast. The front that had passed the previous week had left things perfect. They rode in Sal's 25′ Boston Whaler from a launch at LaPorte and were drifting slowly on Trinity Bay. They used artificial bait exclusively. Little soft plastic shrimp called touts on lead-head jigs or hard plastics that looked like little finfish, festooned with multiple treble hooks. On this day, either proved deadly to the speckled trout. They were filling the ice chest with five-pounders.

"Oh, you said you had a call from Hillman. I been so busy thinking about catching a wall-hanger that I forgot to ask what he wanted," Sal said.

"Seems that state Attorney General guy, Ryley, has gone away. Nobody's seen him for a couple of weeks. I told Hillman not to look at us but just laughed. Seemed to be in a better mood. As we expected, Jack Darling spilled his guts on the esteemed Mr. McDole. And he admitted that the girl had been at his house the night before she jumped. He said McDole's wife was back in Monterey with daddy and ol' *Señor Perez* hadn't made a trip across the border lately. He told me the heroin traffic was back to normal in all the big cities, but they haven't seen any of that in Fayette County."

"Well, maybe we done OK. You done OK. I mean, if you hadn't stayed on this thing, nothing would have happened. Does that make you feel better?" Sal wanted to know.

Doc thought for a minute and said, "Too damn bad

about the girl. Nobody even knows her name, really. Just Victoria." He paused for a beat and went on, "You know, what really gets to me is Darlene. She wasn't a bad person, I don't think. I really enjoyed being with her. She was amazing. And smart. Damn!"

"Yeah, that was a hell of a waste of good talent!"

"Would you quit that shit? The woman is dead. Have a little respect, for Christ's sake."

"I can't help it. She was something special. Damn!"

A few minutes later, Sal had just landed an 8-pounder and was happy. Doc said, "How 'bout you and me hitting some wineries next summer. That would be fun. Lots of free wine."

Sal just looked at him.

THE END

Background on Doc and Fat Sally

I provide the two passages below as background on the relationship between Doc (Connor Quinn) and Fat Sally (Salvatore Lombardo). They have been featured in the "Sanctuary Stories" series. The two were the main male characters in the three-volume novel "Scooter Trash – A Love Story" which was written three years before "The Road to LaGrange". These scenes are from early in the first book of that set — "Thursday's Children." The described events happened in 1972. They also appeared in "The Eagle's Web" but were minor characters.

The first passage described Doc's moving into the shop / bar / home of Albino Bob, the leader of the Sanctuary motorcycle community, following the failure of his marriage.

The second passage covers a meeting between the bikers from Sanctuary as they requested permission from the region's outlaw biker group to start a new motorcycle club.

Hope you enjoy these little snapshots into the friendship of Doc and Sal and that it encourages you to look deeper into the world of Sanctuary and its characters.

***

Doc found Fat Sally and Skinny lounging in Bob's bar. "I'll buy y'all a beer if you help me clean out the spare room upstairs.

"Shit," said Skinny. "That job is worth more than a damn beer."

Sally grabbed Skinny by the arm and said, "Come on, let's give a brother a hand." This was the first time anyone called him "brother"—something meaningful in the biker community.

Skinny grabbed a trashcan from out back and emptied some empty beer cans in another can and dumped the beer dregs on the ground and followed Doc and Sally up the back stairs. They opened the door, and the first impression was the smell—something was dead or rotten in there! There were beer cans and bottles on top of newspapers and dirty abandoned clothes and oily rags and several boxes of trash, a deflated blow-up doll, a flat 21-inch front tire from a bike, old waded-up magazines—Playboy, Hustler, Easy Rider, AMA magazine, bikes for sale advertiser rags and some that were so faded or wadded up that it was impossible to tell. They filled the trash can and hadn't made a dent in the mess—and the smell wasn't getting any better.

"I think there are some of them black plastic trash bags someplace downstairs," said Skinny and he retreated into the hall and let himself take a full breath.

Sally had worked his way across the room and tried to raise the one window in the room, but it was painted shut. He took out his Buck knife and ran it around the frame and finally got it to raise about six inches but stopped when the window frame started to crack and splinter—not enough but better than nothing. He stepped back and did a little jig. "I think I found out where most of the stink is coming from," as he grabbed a greasy rag from the bed and picked up the mostly decomposed body of a sizable rat. Doc handed him a paper bag to put it in and it fell through the bottom and Sally picked it up again and wrapped it in a filthy towel that he found in the corner of the room. Doc was retching and even Sally, who had a cast-iron stomach, was looking a little pale before they got it captured and the bag wrapped tight.

Doc said, "I think Jo must throw all the junk in here when she cleans house."

Skinny heard Doc as he came back with several wadded-up garbage bags. "Well, Jo ain't too big on housework, if you couldn't tell. Gwen tries to give her a hand with cleaning up and sweeping once in a while. And washing the damn dishes."

After a few minutes more, the three finally could see the floor and bed. They had to pick up several dried-up condoms in the final layer of junk—probably from the last time the bed had been used. Doc asked Skinny, "How long has it been since somebody actually used this room?"

"Well, I think a couple of guys passing through about six months ago slept in it—but it was already a mess by then. Them boys weren't too choosy."

They flipped the badly stained mattress, but the other side was just as bad. Blood and grease stains and some others that defied explanation. They tossed the ripped foam pillow that was on the bed. Sweeping the floor and checking the drawers on the dresser was the last chore and they didn't find anything in the drawers but some old hamburger wrappers and some very crusty underwear. Doc said, "I think I can live in here now that most of the stink has cleared out. Hey, Skinny, are there any more of them air fresheners in the bar bathroom—you know the ones for the sign that says 'Don't eat the big Mints'? I could sure use one of them in here for a day or two to hide the rest of the stench."

"I'll see if I can find one but you ain't actually gonna lay on that bed, are you?"

That had crossed Doc's mind. "Hey, Sally, you think the discount store is still open? If you could run me over there, I will pick up some sheets and maybe a plastic tablecloth or something to put over the mattress."

"Alright but this is going to cost you a six-pack. This place was even grosser than I thought." They carried out the bags and the full trashcan and just dumped everything in the burn pit and poured some gas on it and set the whole mess on fire. Good riddance!

Sally didn't go but let Doc drive his Blazer to the local

discount house where he picked up a cheap set of sheets and a fiber-fill pillow—also cheap—and he found something he didn't know existed—a mattress pad with a plastic backing, which was better than a tablecloth. The whole check took over nine bucks from his dwindling stash, but it just might make the room livable.

Doc moved his boxes from the parts room and tried make the bed without touching the mattress—luckily, the mattress pad had fitted corners to hold it on tight and there was a pillowcase with the sheets so his new two-dollar pillow had a cover. Skinny didn't find a fresh mint and didn't want to pull the one out of the urinal but he did find some industrial strength disinfectant and sprayed it liberally throughout the room before Doc got back from his shopping trip. At least the room didn't smell like a dead rat anymore.

Doc went back down to the bar and laid out another $4 for beers for Sally and Skinny and then back up and crashed on his stiff new sheets. He had been wearing work clothes during the clean-up and he thought he should have thrown them in the burn pit. Sleep came fast.

***

It only took about 10 minutes to navigate the empty Sunday streets to the Devil's Jokers' neighborhood. It was on the edge of an industrial area with shabby, post-war houses. It had seen better days. As they turned onto the street, Doc noticed that there were grown-up empty lots and that the only business was a 7-Eleven on the far corner of the block from the clubhouse. "You know, there used to be other houses around here but several mysteriously burned years ago—after Jonesy moved into his place. Other folks just moved out." The house, itself, was a pale green asbestos shingled place, evidently built onto several times, with a double garage separate from the main house. The place looked like it needed a new roof. There were a couple of Harleys in the driveway—one, a full dresser and the other a stripped Electra Glide with a fresh coat of shiny black paint. There was also an old school-bus yellow Dodge panel truck parked half out of the right-side garage bay.

"Y'all know to let me do all the talking. Be friendly but don't make a lot of quick moves—just be respectful and let me handle this." It was evident that Bob was just a little intimidated as they walked to the front door. It was a heavy metal thing with two dead-bolt keyholes. There was a sign in the unkept yard that said *PRIVATE PROPERTY—KEEP OUT.* And there was a banner in the front picture window with the club's logo backed by what appeared to be aluminum foil, blocking any view of the interior.

Bob knocked on the door frame—firmly but not threateningly—only two knocks. In about a minute the locks clicked, and the door opened and there was a short, stocky and weary-looking man in a cut-off jean jacket with Devil's Jokers patches. "Come on in, Bob. You other guys too, come in."

The room was neat with some old but clean living room furniture. In addition to the door man, there were two women standing by a bar to the left side of the room. The bar was just two wooden barrels with what appeared to be a door mounted on top. One of the women was in hip-hugger Levi's and crop top. She was a tall bottle blond with hair piled up and too much make-up. She was probably a real looker a few years ago but the miles were beginning to show. The other woman was skinny with scraggly black hair and a bruise on her chin, and she wouldn't look directly at anyone. They didn't speak but gave little waves without raising their hands. Both were wearing cut-off jackets with property patches. The blonde's patch indicated she belonged to Jonesy and the other one said she was property of Spider.

The door guy said, "Why don't y'all sit down and I will tell Jonesy you are here. It may be a minute—he's on the phone." A patch on the front of his vest said he was the National Vice President and the rocker on the back of his colors identified him as Billy Bob.

The guys plopped down to wait for their audience with the leader—Doc and Bob on one of the couches and Sally in an overstuffed chair. Sally said to the women, "How y'all doing? Anything fun going on around here?"

The women seemed uncomfortable, and the blond said, "We are OK." The skinny chick just turned back toward the bar.

After five minutes, Billy Bob came back in and motioned them to follow him. He led them through the rambling house—most of which looked in good repair and the whole place was clean. They went through the kitchen that that would have served a small café and through what had once been the structure's back door, into a big, dark space which appeared to be the club's meeting room. There was a desk at one end and a scattering of tables and chairs filled the rest of the room. There was a door on the other end of the room which led into a bathroom with the light on. There were posters on the walls—some from movies like "The Wild Bunch" and "Electra Glide in Blue"—and a couple of Nazi posters and a flag with a swastika next to a rebel flag. Behind the desk sat another short, stocky guy. He was clean shaven and had neat hair and what looked to be clean jeans and a black T-shirt under his colors. Beside him stood a taller middle-aged, gray man with a goatee and a bulge on the left side of his cutoff—evidently Spider.

Bob walked confidently over to Jonesy, and they gave each other a big bearhug. Jonesy said, "Pull up some chairs boys and we can catch up a little." They did and Spider stayed as still as stone and Billy Bob walked over and stood behind Jonesy, opposite from Spider. "OK, Bob, who are these boys with you? I think I have seen the big guy before but not the other one."

"Yeah, you know Fat Sally. He was at that rally we went to in the spring. The other one is Doc. He's kind of new to us but he's solid."

Doc was watching and trying to learn how these things work. Sally folded his arms and just assumed a menacing frown, switching his look from Billy Bob to Spider and back. They didn't seem interested.

"Y'all come up alone, Bob?" asked Jonesy.

"Just us and a couple of ol' ladies—they stayed back at the motel while we came here," Bob lied. He didn't want to mention Red.

They had some small talk before getting to business. Turned out that Billy Bob was national VP and also served as the president of the local chapter. Jonesy had enough on his plate without watching out for his local guys. Spider was national sergeant at arms. The Devil's Jokers had eight chapters spread across several states and Jonesy had been a charter member of the first chapter and, through attrition, moved up in the organization over the past 10 years.

"OK, let's get down to it. You want to start a club back home—that's what you told me on the phone. And you don't want it to be a chapter of our club. I can see that. You have always been sort of an ol' lady when it comes to the heat. But that's OK. I don't need another chapter right now."

"Yeah," said Bob. "I'm not looking at nothin' big—just some guys to be a part of something. Most of these guys are just ham-n-eggers. Joe lunchbox guys but they do love to ride and aren't looking to bring down heat or cause anybody misery."

"If I agree with this, we need to get the rules straight from day one. No exceptions. You had a bunch, years back, and they got to stepping on toes and I had to shut it down."

Bob bowed his head a little and said, "Yeah, turned out we had a couple of bad apples and they fucked everything up and I don't blame you for being pissed. We learned from that and none of these boys now had anything to do with any of that. If you agree, I'll make it damn clear what the limits are. I'll put it in the by-laws."

Doc listened and learned. Sally scowled and flexed his arms.

"OK, these are my terms. No slack, no exceptions."

Bob said, "Let's hear it."

"We have an enterprise here and there can't be nothing your group does that gets in the way of that. Period. You don't deal any dope—any kind—grass, pills, acid, heroin, coke—nothing. Your people can use whatever they please but if they sell so much as a lid of grass or one red, the deal is off."

"Understood," said Bob.

"You don't run any women. No truck stop queens, no call girls. More on that in a minute. You don't work security at any festivals, concerts, bike runs or anyplace else. That is a good gig for us, and you can't fuck it up. Absolutely no protection for any businesses. We don't have that going in your area but who knows about someday. And one last thing—no state name on your rocker—town name only. This state is ours."

Bob said, "I think we can live with that. I have one question, though."

"Shoot."

"You said no security or protection. How about guys working as bouncers at bars or after-hours clubs? We have some guys in our area who earn a few extra bucks by picking up some bouncer or door-man work. We also have one potential member who works as a night watchman for a plant. How about that?"

Jonesy thought about it for a minute and looked at Spider for his take. Spider nodded and shrugged. Then Jonesy said., "I ain't looking to take food out of a working man's mouth. I can live with that but if a bouncer gets asked to provide security for a concert or something, he needs to know to turn it down. Also, if you have guys bouncing a club and any of my guys show up, you cut them all the slack they need. Don't want any fights or cops—understand?"

"Sounds good to me, and thanks, guys will appreciate that," said Bob.

"Now, about the women. The Ferret tells me that chick, Kay, turns tricks sometimes. I know she hangs around your place some. There are some other girls in your town who do the same thing. So long as they aren't wearing property patches or aren't affiliated with your club, I don't see a problem, but they can't cross that line. We aren't running any women in your town, but we do hit some of the truck stops along the Interstate and I can't deal with interference. Is that clear."

"Loud and clear. But you are wrong about Kay, regardless of what your guy may tell you. She has some friends who gift her a little but she definitely ain't no hooker. I can guarantee you that."

Doc's fists clinched but he held his cool.

"Ferret says she is one world class piece of ass. I wish I had found out for myself before Ferret got to her. I'd hate to go for his sloppy seconds 'cause there wouldn't be much left," Jonesy laughed.

Doc's fists clinched harder, and he tried not to let his grimace show. He breathed in through his nose and out through his mouth. *No time to fuck up* he told himself. Sally looked at him out of the corner of his eye and shuffled his feet just a little.

Bob said, "Kay ain't nobody's property, anyway. She

is just a friend. And she's no mama, either."

"OK, if are all in agreement, you can go with your little club. You will exist under our nuclear umbrella. No other clubs are going to be stepping on you. What are you going to call it? I need to be OK with that, too."

Bob said, "We have kicked around a couple of things but haven't settled on one. We'll do that in the next week or so and I'll give you a call for your OK."

"Alright. You guys should get on the road if you are gonna get back home before dark." Jonesy's way of telling them the audience was over and to get the hell out of his clubhouse. All six of them walked back through maze that was the house and to the front door. The women were where they were before and no more interested than they were earlier. Bob, Doc and Sally climbed back in the tall Blazer and were headed back to Red's place before 2:30.

Sally grinned and said, "Doc, tell me the Ferret didn't really ruin anything."

Doc let the tension ease and he laughed and said, "I gotta meet that little motherfucker. Far as I can tell there was no damage done. Hey, Bob, are they all a bunch of malignant midgets in that bad-ass club—well, except for Spider?"

"Come to think of it, most of them are little guys. I guess they got slapped around a lot as kids and it just made them mean as hell."

Acknowledgements

This story represents a new direction for me. It is the first crime-based novel I have written. I attempted it after encouragement from several friends. I believe the result is the most readable volume I have penned. For all of their support and suggestions, I would like to thank my great friends Carolyn Junkin, Janet Smith (who will always be Maggie, to me), and Wanda Weber. Thanks to my nephew, Aaron Blackwell, for his review of my early draft of the manuscript and for his thoughtful feedback and suggestions.

Thanks to my sister and cover illustrator, Suzie Blackwell. She is an excellent artist and produces some amazing paintings which continue to be exhibited in various venues in and around Phoenix. She has been very kind and creative in helping in the development of the covers for all of my books. She has given of her time and talent to support an unworthy brother. Love you, baby sister.

Thanks and much love to my daughter, Tonya Jeffery for her support and such great help in marketing and creating images and materials for book signings and for posting on social media. Thanks also for the support of my granddaughters for all their help.

Thanks to my editor, Jesse Coleman, for his leadership and support in getting this and my other works to publication. Without you I'd be lost trying to get my books out.

And, as always, my appreciation and admiration to Jewelz (Betty) Baxter, who is an excellent writer of motorcycle romances and other fine books. You are my hero.

Finally, thanks to the great authors whose works I

devour as soon as they are published. Burke, Sandford, Iles, Baldacci—masters all. These and other fine writers provide me with something to aspire to.

KLM

About the Author

Kerry L. Malone makes his home in League City, Texas. He was born in Texas and raised in Texas and Louisiana, but he has lived in several regions of the country and he has traveled extensively. He holds BS and MEd degrees. Following college, he was a teacher and a football coach and spent several years deeply involved in the biker culture. Afterward he had a long career as an energy industry executive. He has written extensively for professional and personal purposes, as well as some short fiction. "Scooter Trash: A Love Story," written in 2020 was his first novel and he has written several since then. Information about his books and samples of several can be found on his website (author-kerry-malone.net) as well as his Facebook page (Facebook/kerrymalone444) and other social media. All publications are available through Amazon and can be accessed at: www.amzn.to/3Dl3vtW

Made in the USA
Columbia, SC
24 January 2024

30025084R00124